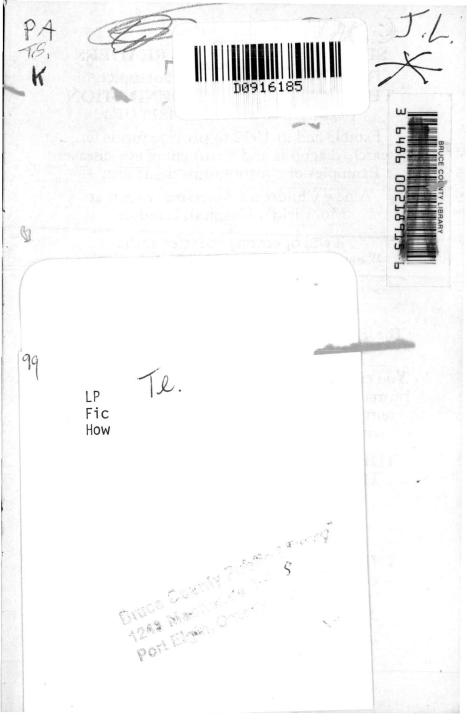

GUNS OF THE PAST

The day Matt Brenner pulled a Peacemaker on Luther Hinton and left the Scarred L Gang, he never looked back — except in nightmares. He settled into the life of a peaceful farmer, but it wasn't long before the outlaw gang — hell bent on revenge — caught up with him. Luther Hinton was never one to leave a score unsettled! Can Matt escape and save the woman he loves, or will he become the victim of his past mistakes?

LANCE HOWARD

GUNS OF THE PAST

Complete and Unabridged

LINFORD
Leicester

First published in Great Britain in 1997 by
Robert Hale Limited
London

First Linford Edition
published 1998
by arrangement with
Robert Hale Limited
London

British Library CIP Data

Howard, Lance
    Guns of the past.—Large print ed.—
Linford western library
1. Western stories
2. Large type books
I. Title
823.9′14 [F]

ISBN 0–7089–5371–9

Published by
F. A. Thorpe (Publishing) Ltd.
Anstey, Leicestershire

Set by Words & Graphics Ltd.
Anstey, Leicestershire
Printed and bound in Great Britain by
T. J. International Ltd., Padstow, Cornwall

This book is printed on acid-free paper

To all who have suffered the injustice of racism and abuse . . . and again to George Baker for great music and inspiration.

1

A bullet shattered the farmhouse window. Glass imploded, shards glittering, spiralling in all directions, raining on to the threadbare parlor carpet.

Morning. The sun peeked over the horizon, splashing topaz light across the rugged Colorado landscape. Fields glowed emerald green and, far distant, the blue, snow-capped Rockies sparkled diamond and sapphire. The gems of morning, John Brenner liked to call them. A peaceful time, when all the world was reborn and the lonely hauntings of the night melted away.

A peaceful time.

Except for the bullet that blasted the window to smithereens and murdered the serenity, and brought unpaid debts and unforgiven affronts to mind.

'Judas Priest!' blurted John Brenner,

who entered the parlor just as the bullet obliterated the window. His cup of Arbuckle's jumped from his hand, joining the window in shattered pieces on the floor. Brown liquid splashed out in a bloodsplatter pattern and he stared at the mess, eyes narrowed and heart thudding.

'What the hell was that?' snapped Tim Brenner, vaulting from a hard-backed chair near the fireplace. Shock jumping on to his young face, he peered at his uncle, looking for answers John could not provide — or was that *hoped* he'd never have to give?

Instead of answering, John slowly shook his head. His blue eyes narrowed to a squint, gaze lifting to the window. 'Galldamned if I know . . . ' Did another lie matter? He reckoned Hell was all one direction and one step more or less wouldn't make much of a difference.

Tim Brenner moved over to him, face creased with worry. 'Maybe it was an accident? Maybe someone out

2

huntin' or target shootin'?'

John forced himself to move, sweeping out a hand and pushing the younger Brenner out of the line of the window in case another shot followed. He had a powerful gut feeling one would. 'Who'd be out shooting this time of the mornin'?' His voice came subdued, edged with resignation. Who'd be out shooting, indeed.

The younger Brenner shrugged, running a hand through his dirty-blond hair and crinkling his brow. 'Never know. Some early riser — '

'Don't be ridiculous!' John snapped, words cracking with more force than he intended. The shot had rattled him, but his irritation went deeper than that. Years deeper. A feeling, a foreboding sense of doom, of vendettas unfinished, revisited, chilled him. What else could it be? In the five years they'd lived in Colorado they had never encountered a lick of trouble. Stray bullets just didn't happen this far from town. They, his younger brother, Matt, and nephew,

Tim, were peaceful farmers now, trying to make a new start.

You can't start over — he won't let you! You knew this day would come and you ignored it, you foolish sonofabitch! Now you'll pay the price.

'Jesus H.!' he muttered, the thought startling him as much as the bullet. Something dark had come back, returned for its due and now there was only facing it, paying the debt.

With chilling certainty, John knew that shot would not be the last.

As his gaze focused on Tim he saw hurt in the youth's eyes and felt guilt rise. Cursing himself for his harsh rebuke, he said in a weak voice, 'Sorry . . . didn't mean to take your head off.'

Tim's face softened. 'Godamighty, John, didn't mean anything by it. Just scared, is all.'

John gave his nephew a smile that was far less reassuring than he wished. 'That shot got me boogered, too. I'm sure it was no accident.'

Tim's brow arched and surprise

danced in his eyes. 'You think it was on purpose?'

John gave a slow nod, a grim look filtering on to his features. 'I got a powerful bad notion all hell's about to break loose.'

All hell did break loose. Suddenly, like a barrage of Rocky Mountain thunder, a hellstorm. A volley of shots blasted in staccato rhythm, earsplitting, soulrattling. Bullets thunked into the planks of the outside wall and whined through the window opening. John caught sight of blue gunsmoke clouds, drifting lazily across the yard, meandering wraiths. Glass jangled as another window disintegrated under a hail of lead.

John shoved Tim back and the boy dove, coming up beside a wall, back pressed to the boards. His face twisted in fear and John felt guilt knot his belly. The boy had never experienced the horrors he and his brother had, the terror of flying lead, the coppery, sour stench of blood, the grotesque mockery of wrongful death. They had done their damnedest to shield him from it, from their past, but perhaps that had been a mistake. Perhaps if they hadn't taken it upon themselves to protect the boy he'd be better prepared.

John had scant time to dwell on it. The world was blistering around him. He dived for the gun cabinet in the corner, throwing open the glass doors and snapping up his best Winchester. He jammed a full load into its chamber and whirled, crouching as he scooted for the window.

Lead shrieked through the opening, punching into floorboards and walls. Twenty bullets must have buried themselves in the woodwork before he reached the window. Whoever was firing was doing it with deadly intent and purpose, though not to kill, no, not just yet. Just to frighten, to serve notice the Devil had returned to collect their souls, souls he and Matt had signed away five years ago on a sunny Kansas morning.

He's back . . .

God help us . . .

In the back of his mind, John had always known this day would come, though God in Heaven he'd spent years denying it. Denying death. He reckoned Matt had, too.

It was time to pay for the sins of the past.

In blood.

As he crouched near the window, shoulder jammed to the wall, he felt glad of only one thing: Matt was in town. Perhaps he would have a chance to escape, perhaps he would somehow have enough warning. For that's who the madness, the dark force, had come for: Matt. The Devil in the form of a man had come for Matt.

The shooting came to an abrupt halt. A stunned silence followed and blue smoke genies drifted across the yard. They waited, throwing glances at one another, hearts pounding.

'What's happenin', John?' Tim's voice trembled. 'What in the goddamn hell's happenin'?'

John shook his head and let out a prolonged sigh. Sweat beaded on his brow and trickled into his eyes, stinging. It was time to come clean with the boy; he had no choice. He looked at Tim, defeat and guilt haunting his eyes. 'Matt and I weren't completely honest with you 'bout some things, son. I know we were wrong, now, dead wrong, but that won't change the fact that someone we knew a long time ago has come back to claim his due.'

'Who, John? Who's come back? What does he want?'

'The who ain't important, but he wants Matt, more'n likely. He wouldn't have much use for us.'

'That mean he won't kill us?' There was a bit of selfishness in the boy's question and John couldn't blame him.

John's lips drew tight. 'Wish I could say it did. But this man . . . this man, he ain't the merciful type. When folks get in his way he removes them.'

A startled look darkened Tim's face. 'He'll kill us?'

John closed his eyes, slowly reopening them. 'Son, I reckon that's in the hands of God, now.'

An unreadable look sprang into Tim's eyes and he leaped up, dashing for the gun cabinet and grabbing a Winchester. Loading it, he ran back to his spot by the window and levered a shell into the chamber.

He stared at his uncle, a demeanor of seriousness coming on to his face that made him look twenty years older, a mature man instead of a sixteen-year-old boy. 'I'm helpin', John. I ain't dyin' no coward, no goddamn way.'

John's face turned more grim but he felt his respect for his nephew grow. 'You know damn little 'bout shootin', son. You'll get yourself killed.' It was a stupid thing to say and John knew as much, but he could think of nothing better.

'I'll shorely get myself killed waitin' on whoever's out there!'

John peered at him, admiring the courage of the young man he and Matt had practically raised over the last five years. The boy had been orphaned when his ma and pa were butchered in a Blackfeet raid, and they had taken him in, brought him up the best they knew how and, pride be damned, they hadn't done half bad. But what had they raised him for? This? To die like a butchered beast when the past caught up with them? Didn't Tim deserve more?

Yes, but it was too late to argue something he had no power to change. He only hoped this once God would show them mercy. But he doubted it.

John gave the boy a forced smile and peeked out the window, trying to get an idea which direction the attack was coming from. He caught vague sounds, hushed voices, chambers clacking as they were reloaded, whispered orders and the swish of clothing, the muffled thud of bootheels. The attackers were manoeuvring closer. He knew it, *felt* it. They were manoeuvring closer and soon they would be on them.

How many?

He didn't know, at least three from the shots, maybe four, maybe five. Five would be right if everything had stayed the same, but it mattered little because he and Tim were outnumbered and outgunned, and if he knew who was out there, outskilled. The man stalking them was a master of sudden violent death and even Lucifer himself would have been hard-pressed to best him.

'Luther . . . ' John mumbled, and Tim stared at him, wide-eyed.

'Hinton?' the boy asked with a gasp, terror springing into his voice. 'Christamighty, John, I didn't know it was that bad!'

John gave a forced nod. No use denying it. 'Sorry to say, son, the past has come a-callin'.'

'Callin' us out . . . ' The boy's voice dropped, defeated. 'We got no chance.'

'The hell we don't! We're Brenners;

we always got a chance. My brother and I come through worse than this, so have you. We'll make it.' He tried to sound forceful, confident, but his voice betrayed him.

'Sure we will, John. Sure we will.' Tim's voice held no conviction; it was the tone of a man who'd lost faith.

The silence made John's nerves raw. It seemed suddenly worse than the roar of gunfire. At least when bullets flew they knew what was happening, where the enemy lay. His fingers tightened on the rifle stock, knuckles bleaching, tendons standing out like white rawhide straps.

He couldn't take it any longer. He had to do something, anything, or go loco. He poked the rifle out the window and triggered a shot. A useless move, but it provided him a meagre sense of control.

The bullet ploughed into empty ground and a harsh laugh, filled with contempt and mockery, echoed across the yard. John tensed. A chill travelled the length of his spine. His worst fears were confirmed. He recognized that laugh, though he'd encountered the man only once. He reckoned he would have known that laugh even if he'd never heard it.

It was the laugh of death.

'Judas Priest, John!' blurted Tim. 'He's got a laugh like a goddamned coyote!'

'Even a coyote's got more honor and mercy than that man, son. Luther Hinton's a man without a soul.'

As if in reply, a second volley of shots blasted from unseen guns. Spits of flame stabbed the air and clouds of blue smoke tumbled across the yard. Lead shrieked through the windows, coming dangerously close to John's head. He jerked back, breath catching in his throat. Sweat streamed down his face and he swore his heart would burst through his chest any minute.

You're going to die!

The thought made things worse and he pushed it from his mind. Perhaps not, he struggled to convince himself. Perhaps he'd get lucky with a bullet, or perhaps Matt would realize what had happened and escape; perhaps God in Heaven would this once look upon the Brenners with His favor. Slim hope, but better than none at all.

Lead ploughed into boards, tearing furrows in the carpet, embedding in walls. Vases exploded as slugs hit them, fragments raining to the floor.

The shots stopped. Again.

Tim's voice, high and breaking, cracked in the stunned silence. 'What the hell's he doin'?'

John glanced at the boy, who was trembling visibly, eyes darting back and forth.

John gave him a sombre shake of his head. 'He likes to torment his prey 'fore he swallows it. That's his way.'

Tim shook his head. 'I ain't never felt this scared before, John, and I ain't afraid to admit it.'

'No shame in that, son. Just means you're a man, surely it does.'

14

A thin smile turned Tim's lips and he jumped up and shoved his rifle through the opening, intending to trigger a shot at anything.

He never pulled the trigger.

Two things happened in almost the same breath: a thunderous crash sounded and the back door burst open. Three men brandishing six-shooters, all levelled waist high, crowded through. Shock jumping on to his face, John whirled to meet the attack. But before he could fire the lead man's gun swung his way and flame snapped from the barrel.

The slug tore through John's shoulder, sending him slamming into the wall behind him. The Winchester spun from his grip, landing on the floor a few feet away and discharging; the bullet buried itself harmlessly in a wall and the recoil kicked the rifle across the parlor.

At the instant Tim poked his rifle through the window, hands seized the barrel and jerked, wrenching it from his grip. Dumbfounded, the youth peered

15

at his empty hands. A man jumped from beneath the window and laughed, twirling the rifle in his grip and clacking Tim in the face with the butt.

Tim stumbled back, blood spraying from his mouth. He clutched his jaw, teeth ringing with pain, and went down, landing heavily on his seat. The man who grabbed the rifle dove out of sight, reappearing with another man a moment later at the back door.

The man who walked in beside the hardcase who had grabbed the rifle stepped to the front. He was a sight, this man, a sight only those close to death generally laid eyes on. He was the Reaper himself, far as John was concerned, a figure of darkness and greed, devoid of mercy and compassion. Inhuman. As much a monster as a man could be. Not a large man, as standards went, but wide and muscular. His duster swished about his legs as he walked forward. His boots clomped hollowly on the floorboards. His gaze was piercing, the color of horseshoe metal, as empty of emotion as a man could get. A winding scar started at his forehead and arced to the corner of one eye. A low-pulled battered felt hat shadowed his face, the aquiline nose and thin bloodless lips. Tangled black hair half-covered one eye and greasy strands touched his shoulders. The hair was thin, patchy in places, infested with lice, scalp crusty with scabs.

The man stepped closer, hand slipping over the tooled leather holster at his hip. The image of a dragon was seared into the leather, the craftwork of 'some Chinaman', as Luther used to call him, to whom he had delivered swift death as payment.

'Long time no see, John,' Luther said, a grin slipping over his thin lips. His eyes narrowed as he peered at John, gaze settling on the wound at his shoulder. 'Nasty wound you got there, *mi amigo*. Reckon you'd die from that if'n you didn't get some attention. Course, you won't get the chance.'

The outlaw took another step forward and grabbed a handful of John's shirt, hauling him around and hurling him to the floor. He walked over and kicked him in the teeth. Blood sprayed from John's mouth, sprinkling the floor, and he groaned.

Luther Hinton kneeled, joints cracking. 'Christ, John, you know how I hate to muss up my boots. You co-operate and I won't have to kick ya 'g'in.' He laughed, a demonic sound. He *was* the Devil. His eyes showed nothing that even hinted at humanity, just an insane vacant light, a gleeful madness —

'You *bastard*!'

The cry snapped John's thoughts short. It came sharp and sudden as Tim Brenner vaulted to his feet, diving at the outlaw leader. Luther sprang up, trying to swing his gun around, but didn't make it in time. Tim hit him in mid-whirl, knocking him back a pace.

'You leave him be!' Tim shouted, pounding his fists against the outlaw's chest, blood dribbling from his own mouth. His fists seemed sorely inadequate for the task, bouncing off the outlaw, who blinked, insane fire burning cold in his eyes.

The other four men watched with bemused curiosity, none making a move to lend a hand. Luther Hinton needed no help and would have shot the first one who offered.

Tim clouted the outlaw across the face and Hinton scoffed, mocking his efforts.

Hinton pistoned a blow to the youth's chest that twisted the boy around and propelled him backward with the force of a gunshot. He slammed into a wall face-first, rebounding and crashing to the floor flat on his back. Dazed, he stared up at the ceiling.

The outlaw stepped over to him, gazing at the stunned look in the boy's eyes. He drew his Smith & Wesson, levelling on the boy and cocking the hammer in a prolonged *skriiik*.

'You got sand, boy. I hate that.'

'No!' John screamed, turning on to

his stomach and thrusting out his hand. 'Luther, please . . . please don't hurt him! He ain't done nothin' to you.'

Luther turned, eyes narrowing as they centered on John. 'One Brenner done somethin' to me, all done somethin' to me.' He turned back to the boy, who was staring up with a look of utter terror. An evil smile oiled Luther's lips but he eased the hammer back, holstering his gun. 'You're lucky I'm in a good mood 'cause I found your brother, boy. Else your life mighta ended a few minutes sooner than it will.'

Luther motioned to the men at the back, who stepped deeper into the room.

He looked at one of them and said, 'Get a rope from one of the horses and bring it here.' The fellow, Rico, a Mex with stringy black hair and a missing left pinkie, scurried out, returning a moment later with a coil of rope.

Two of the other men, as if by

unspoken command, grabbed hard-backed chairs and dragged them to the center of the room, turning them to face each other, leaving a good five feet between. Luther nodded to John and Tim and the men hauled them to the chairs. Using Bowie knives, they cut lengths of rope and lashed John and Tim's hands together behind the chairs.

John's head drooped and he struggled to lift it, meeting the metallic vacant eyes of the outlaw leader.

'What . . . what do you want, Luther? We got nothin' for you no more. It was a long time ago.'

'You're right, about that, *amigo*. Was a long time ago. Five goddamn years or more, I reckon. But I never forget. Matt shoulda known that. Once you're part of my gang, you're signed up for life. I got no retirement plan.'

'Please, leave us be. You can take whatever you want. We're just peaceful farmers, now. We don't want no trouble.'

Fury exploded in Luther's horseshoe-colored eyes. He lashed out, the back of his hand striking John full across the face. John's head rocked and his senses turned hazy. The room gyrated, steadied abruptly. 'You got trouble, farmer man. You got trouble the day you walked into my camp and helped your no-good brother get away! You got trouble the day you drew that gun on me and made me throw mine in that stream. You got trouble the day you laid eyes on Luther Hinton!'

John shook his head in useless protest, the certainty of death flooding his eyes. Hinton was worse now, if that were possible. Plumb crazy loco. John saw it plain on the outlaw's face. There would be no appeasing him, except with blood. 'We got nothin' you want, Luther. We're done with the past.'

Luther bellowed a laugh. 'So you count your losses and think you can just go on your merry way and live a nice peaceful life; that it, Brenner?'

John's eyes shifted but he remained silent.

Luther leaned in, grabbing the chair arms. 'How many folks in these parts know what your brother done, Brenner? How many? Reckon none. Reckon a fella like Matt don't rightly want to admit he knows Luther Hinton and the Scarred L Gang, does he? Reckon folks might look at him a bit closer, maybe find out some things that don't match up with the peaceable farmer he pretends to be.'

'Go to hell, you sonofabitch!'

Hinton's eyes grew chilled and he shook both arms of the chair, leaning closer to John. John could smell the outlaw's sour breath, the rancid odor of his person. He smelled like a coyote, mangy, a scavenger who fed on the corpses of others. 'How you buy this farm, John? Where'd you get the money?' John's gaze shifted; he couldn't bear to look at the outlaw any longer.

'Don't owe you no explanation.'

'No? I got a feelin' I know. Matt took somethin' from me that day, John. I want it back.'

John's fright got the better of him. He couldn't stand the outlaw's gaze on him, his sour smell or his close proximity. 'Goddammit, Luther, that was five years ago! It's gone! He ain't got it no more!'

Luther gave a spiteful laugh. 'Good; you know what I'm gettin' at.'

'I know. But you're wrong. He ain't got it no more.'

'You best pray he does, for his sake.'

'You'll kill me whether I tell or not. Then you'll kill Matt.'

Luther cocked an eyebrow. 'There's no repentance for what you done, John. You know that. I've already passed judgment. But Matt . . . well, maybe I ain't quite decided.'

'You're lyin'. You decided 'fore you came here. You'd never let him live. It ain't in your make-up.'

Luther's face turned stony and he

drew back, going to the window, staring out across the yard while running a finger across his lips. John waited, the silence thick and ominous, the men with Luther not moving an inch from where they stood, nor making any sound. They watched in sullen compliance, knowing the consequences of interfering.

Luther turned from the window. 'You and Matt buy this spread with my money, John? I help you out with that? That why Matt don't have it?'

John's eyes narrowed. 'We bought this spread on our own. Worked for it with our own blood and tears. We ain't the same as the likes of you. We don't take what ain't ours. We build our own.'

Luther uttered a thin laugh. 'Then what'd he do with it? Give it to the poor, maybe?' His voice came low, threatening in its very calmness, then suddenly it leaped into a shout. *'Build a goddamned church where he could save his worthless soul?'* Luther stepped across the floor and snapped out his gun, jamming it against John's forehead, clenching it so tight his hand turned white. 'Where is it, John!' he shouted, insanity in his eyes. '*Where the goddamn hell is it?*'

'Please,' John mumbled, feeling the pain of the barrel pressing hard into his forehead. He saw his life flowing away and said a silent prayer as he looked into the eyes of death. 'Please, don't kill me . . .'

Luther's eyes glittered and something lived within them that terrified John to his very soul, something hideous and twisted and cruel. 'Why, I ain't gonna kill you, John, not till you give me what I want.'

Luther suddenly pulled the Smith & Wesson away from John's forehead, leaving a round white indentation in the flesh. ''Course, the boy I ain't rightly got no more use for!'

'*Nooooo!*' John screamed, struggling furiously against the ropes as the gun came to aim on Tim. His heart hammered with the utter uselessness of his struggle. He couldn't stop what was coming. God in Heaven he couldn't stop it!

Luther aimed at Tim's head and the boy's eyes widened in stark terror. Luther squeezed the trigger with malicious reverence. The shot thundered in the small room and Tim Brenner jerked, the force of the bullet drilling into his forehead sending the chair over backwards. He thudded back on to the floor, legs in the air, twitching, then going still. He stared sightlessly at the ceiling, the terror frozen in his eyes.

'Jesus, God, no Luther!' John cried, tears rushing from his eyes. His heart seemed to stop, crushed by sorrow and loss. The utter viciousness of the attack shocked even him. Luther had always been mean but the years had deteriorated any ounce of humanity the man might have had, if he had ever truly had any at all. For the boy, the terror was ended. He was free. And only the living were left to suffer.

Luther stared at the dead boy a moment then stepped over to John, face holding a vile expression. He heaved John out of his chair and hurled him sideways. John crashed into the fireplace, the brick tearing a patch of flesh from his cheek and sending an explosion of stars across his vision. His legs went out from under him and he hit the floor, only half aware that he was still alive.

The thunder of Luther's voice pierced his dazed mind. 'I want what's mine, Brenner!' The outlaw stepped over to him and hoisted him up, jamming him against the wall. He pressed his face close and John, vision blurred and jittery, struggled to focus on it. Tears and blood streamed down his face.

Hot emotion cascaded from his being, hate, fury, bitterness. 'You sonofabitch! You goddamn loco sonofabitch!' John spat, catching Luther in the face and the outlaw whirled him around and sent him flying backwards. He went over the arm of the sofa and crashed into the floor at the feet of the men standing in silent watch. One looked at him, a persimmon smile on his face.

Luther stepped forward again and stooped, grabbing John's chin and pulling his face up. 'I'm runnin' out of patience, Brenner. I want what Matt took from me. Now!'

The fight had drained out of John. He struggled to make his lips work. 'He . . . he don't have it, Luther. I swear to God he don't.'

Luther's eyes narrowed. 'Then I want him. Where is he?'

'He's . . . he's gone. He left for Montana last week. Had some . . . business up there.'

Luther Hinton scoffed and spat on the floor. 'You don't rightly expect me to believe that hogwash? You know better'n that.'

John hadn't expected the outlaw to swallow the story, but he had hoped to buy time, grasp at the thread of a chance he'd be left alive to warn Matt, alert him before the outlaw found him.

A fleeting, useless hope.

'*Where is he?*' Luther shouted, thudding John's head against the floor.

John's mind spun and stunning pain sent a cloud of blackness across his thoughts. He gurgled something unintelligible and Luther stood, disgust and fury on his face. He motioned to Rico, who quickly stepped over and heaved John Brenner back into his chair.

'Tie him to it. Don't want him gettin' loose and warnin' his brother.'

Rico quickly complied, lashing John to the chair.

Luther went to the mantle and picked up a kerosene lantern. He brought it over and held it in front of John, lifting off the chimney and setting it on a table. He plucked a lucifer from his pocket and struck it on a tooth. He watched the flame a moment, as if fascinated by whatever bastard notion lived in his mind. John, head partially clear, looked up through bleary eyes, the outlaw leader's face jumping and hazy before his vision. He no longer cared what the leader did to him. His life was over and he didn't give a damn now how he died. Only that Matt somehow escaped, somehow was able to live the life he deserved, the life he had strived so hard for over the past five years. But Luther Hinton would never let the past rest and John's thin lie had not dissuaded him; it would not send him on a wrong trail. He would find Matt in town and then . . .

Luther touched the match to the wick and the lamp burst to light. He turned up the flame until it wavered like a blurry firebrand before John's eyes.

'Say howdy to the Devil for me, John. An' don't you worry none, me and Matt will have a right fine talk when I find him. And I will find him. Then I'll send him to visit ya.'

Luther hurled the lamp. It shattered against the wall with an explosive *woof*!

Kerosene splashed the wall and floor and flames leaped across the boards. It spread quickly; in seconds half the wall was aflame.

Luther's laugh rose above the crepitation of flames and he watched, transfixed by the fiery tongues a moment then motioned for his men to follow him out. John sat alone in the parlor, alone with death. The heat blistered the flesh of his hands and face. Smoke choked his lungs and he coughed, pain lancing his chest. He struggled for breath, strangling. In his last seconds of life he said a prayer for Matt, knowing it would surely take an act of God to save his brother.

An act he had little faith would come.

* * *

Outside the outlaws gathered a few hundred feet from the farmhouse. They watched as the place burst into flames, dry wood being gobbled like tinder. Black smoke billowed from windows and flames stabbed the morning sky.

Luther uttered a harsh laugh, firing his gun into the air and holstering it. One of his men, a man with a gaunt face and hollow eyes and a hoarse moist cough named Jetter, stepped up to him. 'What now, Luther? We don't have Matt.'

'Will soon enough.'

'Think so?' The man shuddered with a violent cough, sweating profusely. His face went a shade paler. The dark circles about his eyes seemed to deepen. He wiped phlegm mixed with specks of blood on his shirt sleeve.

Luther glanced at him, a peculiar expression pulling at one side of his lips. 'Christ, Jetter, any day your lungs gonna come out your mouth. I should shoot ya and put you out of my misery. You'll give us all the consumption you keep hackin' that way.'

The man's rheumy eyes took on a frightened look and he fought to suppress his tubercular cough.

Luther laughed. 'Don't worry, Jetter. You'll die on your own long before I take a serious notion to bury ya.'

Two other men peered at Luther. Both resembled the outlaw in many ways, though younger. Both had faces more at home on Wanted posters than church bulletins and neither was likely to commit an act of kindness anytime soon. Black stringy hair hung limply to their shoulders and each had a smile stained by browned jagged teeth and soured by old tobacco and rotgut whiskey. Bart and Jed Hinton, the remaining members of the Scarred L Gang, were, in fact, Luther's brothers.

'He said Matt went to Montana.' Jed Hinton spat and swiped a backhand across his wet lips, leaving a brown stain across his knuckles.

'He was lyin' to protect him, you idiot.' Luther's eyes remained fixed on the inferno that was the farmhouse. 'He's here, somewhere, I can feel him. All we gotta do is find him.'

'In town?' asked Bart. The outlaw brother fished a paper and tobacco out of a shirt pocket and rolled a smoke. Pungent Durham drifted with the scent of charred wood and a stronger sweet-rotten odor that likely belonged to burning flesh and muscle.

'Reckon.'

'We gonna go kill him?' Jed looked hopeful.

' 'Course we are, but first we're gonna make him suffer and tell us what he done with it.'

'How?' asked Rico, eyes dark and grim.

'Let him find his farm after I have a little parley with him.' He smiled. 'That'll just be the start of it.'

The men laughed and went to their horses, mounting. Luther watched the house cave in on itself, feeling immensely satisfied. He had waited five years for this moment and no one would deny him the pleasure of gloating.

As Luther stared at the flames, a

thought crossed his mind. He would need to change his head-on style for a spell in order to torture Matt Brenner. He would rather kill the sonofabitch outright for disgracing him those years back, making a fool out of him in front of his men. But that would be too easy, the thrill fleeting. This way would be better. Taunt the *hombre*, pull off his wings, make him see before he died that no man did that to Luther Hinton and walked away scot free. No man.

No, Matt Brenner would suffer, and he would tell what he had done with Luther's property before he died for his deeds. He would tell even if he no longer had it, because the object wasn't the point, it was just the frosting on the cake, to Luther's way of thinking. It had taken five years to track Brenner from Kansas — the boy had been so careful not to leave a trail, but no man exists without leaving something behind — Luther would not be denied the pleasure of watching him beg for mercy, plead for his goddamn pitiful life.

A snap like a gunshot sounded from the remains of the house and a great spray of sparks and flame shot into the air. The blue sky blackened momentarily with smoke.

Luther went to his horse and climbed into the saddle, reining around. He peered at his men, indicating the corral full of horses to the left, the barn to the right. 'Finish it!'

The men let out whoops and yahs and drew their guns, firing into the air as they raced towards the corrals. One leaped from his horse and threw open the gate and horses, whinnying and spooked, bolted through the opening, scattering.

Rico and Jed attended to the barn, dashing inside and locating kerosene canisters, dousing the boards. They set the barn aflame, and remounted, watching the results from a safe distance.

When it was done, Luther surveyed

the devastation, an evil smile returning to his lips.

'What now, Luther?' asked Jed, peering at his brother.

Luther's smile widened. 'Now, we go to town . . .'

2

On a day like today a man could almost forget the past, Matt Brenner thought, as he drew his buckboard to a halt in front of the general store.

And the past was something he'd tried so desperately to forget over the last five years.

At times he would forget. Almost. But not quite, and that's what caused him the most regret, that he couldn't assuage all the guilt weighting his soul. He reckoned he never would be free of it completely. There was only carrying on, letting it dwell at the back of his thoughts, the occasional nightmare, and atoning in the only way he knew how.

That's what he aimed to do after he got some supplies — atone. For indiscretions, for past sins, for the stupidities committed in youth. When he finished at the general store, he would walk over to the bank, the way he did every third Monday, and wire a sum of cash to a family in Kansas, a family without a father. The cash was transferred anonymously, though God knew he wanted to put his name to it, accept the guilt, the pain he'd caused them, though rightly that guilt was shared. He always decided against it in the end and sometimes he cursed himself for being a coward at heart. John assured him he wasn't, that it was best for all concerned, because to admit guilt to the family would provide a possible trail one man would follow to the ends of the earth, a trail that could only end in misconceived vengeance and more death.

The sun blazed just above the horizon, splashing its golden light through the streets of the small Colorado town of Hopespring. It glistened from dewcoated hitch rails and sparkled from water troughs and rain barrels, glinted from windows. The dust-and manure-coated Main Street looked gilded, as if it were a street in Heaven and he smiled a smile that came with only a hint of some past sadness. Hopespring was not a large town, merely a circular affair of buildings and a handful of streets. General store, marshal's office, livery, scattered shops and businesses — nothing to set it apart from any other town in Colorado Territory, and that's what Matt appreciated most. They would never find him here, in a no-name settlement tucked in the Colorado wilds. At least that's what he told himself again and again, though men such as that had a knack for showing up when you least wanted them to. Men like that came on like the consumption, a black disease, leaving whatever they touched ravaged, eaten away, forcing those who were left behind to suffer with the consequences and cruel memories.

Sometimes it was better to die. Better to escape than live with a nightmare.

*What the tarnation are you doin'
thinkin' that way this fine mornin'?*
He had to wonder, but then not
too much. He always thought of
the past when he made his monthly
wire. The very act drew out the
poison, the same as when he stripped
down at night and felt the hideous
Scarred L knife-branded on to his
left breast. Reminders. Everywhere.
Reminders that would haunt him till
the day he died.

Matt Brenner shook his head and
sighed a heavy sigh. He climbed from
the seat of his buckboard and secured
the horse to the hitch rail. He regretted
he would have to ask Mr Fuller to front
him for a few weeks. The farm had
been running a little short lately but
things would pick up soon. He had that
money in the bank, but it was not his
to spend. The price of sin was high.

Crossing the boardwalk, he stepped
into the store. Sunlight spilled across
the dusty floor and glinted from canned
goods stacked on shelves. His gaze

scanned the shop, selecting the things he would need.

'Top of the mornin' to ye, lad!' Mr Fuller said from behind the counter that ran along the right wall. An effusive grin spread his lips and sandy eyebrows arched, blue eyes twinkling beneath.

Matt tipped his hat and smiled an easy smile. ' 'Fraid I got a favor to ask you, Mr Fuller, and I ain't proud of the fact.' Matt lifted his hat and brushed sandy-brown hair from his forehead. His face possessed a rugged character, though creased with premature lines about the eyes and mouth that made him look somewhat beyond his thirty-two years.

Worry did that to a man.

So did guilt. But he rightly didn't care. He had no one to impress. He was handsome, at least a few ladies in town had told him as much, though he had never been inclined to court one. He doubted he would at this point and supposed it didn't matter much. A man could grow used to loneliness. He was a little over average height, muscular and browned by days working under the hot sun.

He walked to the counter, stride easy and controlled. Leaning against it, his hazel eyes settled on the shopkeep.

'Name it, lad.' The shopkeep's face was ruddy, crinkled and creased, as if crows had walked across it and left their tracks. Red hair toppled over a large forehead. He had a nose peppered with freckles and veined by too close an acquaintance with Dr Whiskey, but an affable nature and generous spirit Matt admired.

'Whelp, seems we're a bit on the short side again and I need some grain and such. Was hopin' you could spot me. Promise I'll make it up to you.'

The 'keep waved a hand. 'Don't ye worry about it, lad. Ye know I trust ye and yer kin like they was my own — how long we talkin'?'

Matt rubbed his chin, considering. 'Week, maybe two at the most.'

'Pick out what ye need and I'll tally it up.'

'Much obliged.' Matt tipped his hat then turned and went to the shelves, selecting a few can goods and sacks of grain. He piled them by the counter. Lastly he picked out a box of cigars, a present for John's birthday next week.

The 'keep eyed him with a curious, steady gaze, and Matt smiled. Mr Fuller was sort of like the uncle he'd never had. He watched over Tim when Matt brought him to town, had pulled the boy out of a scrape once or twice, even rescuing him from the clutches of a bargirl with dubious notions on her mind.

The 'keep continued to stare and cleared his throat and Matt gave him a raised eyebrow. 'Somethin' tells me you got somethin' on your mind, Mr Fuller.'

'Ah, lad, ye know me too well, ye do.'

'Then out with it, you old sidewinder.' Matt thunked both elbows on the countertop and peered across at the 'keep.

Mr Fuller grinned and his blue eyes twinkled mischievously. 'Well, I got me to thinkin' when I was over the good Widow Farlaw's place the other night — now nothing improprietous, mind you, just a wee bit of dinner and maybe a nip of the good old Scotch whisky. She's a fine cook, lad, the widow is. A fine cook.'

Matt lifted the corner of his mouth in a crooked grin. He had a notion he knew what was coming. 'Don't say? Bet she's good at more than cookin', Mr Fuller.'

The 'keep's cheeks tinted a shade redder than normal and his eyes roved. 'Well, she is a woman of multiple charms, shall we say.'

'We shall say.' His grin widened.

Mr Fuller cleared his throat in an exaggerated manner. 'Well, like I was sayin', I was at her house havin' me a wee nip of Scotch when lo and behold who should walk in . . . ?'

Matt frowned. 'I'm afraid to ask.'

'Ye shouldn't be, lad. T'was her daughter, no less.'

The frown deepened. 'No less.'

'She's prettier than a loch in the sunlight, she is for a fact, lad. And she can cook, so I hear tell.'

'Who told you, the Widow Farlaw?'

'Why, yes, lad, she sure did! Said her lassie could cook almost as fine as herself.'

Matt grunted. 'Way I recollect it, looked like none of that cookin' had gone anywhere but her hips.'

'Well, she is a wee bit on the plump side. I prefer to think of her as a stout gal with plenty of heart.'

'Didn't she take a shotgun to one of her beaux 'bout six months back, when she caught him upstairs at the saloon?' Matt cocked an eyebrow.

'Well, see, lad, that was all just a big misunderstandin', that's all it t'was.'

'Some misunderstandin'. Spent the night in the hoosegow.'

'Well, she had every right, lad. That

fella was cheatin' on her with one o' Miss Molly's gals. How would it be to have your prospective husband spendin' his time, er, tryin' out other wares, shall we say.'

Matt laughed and shook his head. 'Thanks but no thanks, Mr Fuller. My life's peaceable at the moment and I aim to keep it such.'

'You don't know what you're passin' up, lad. She's a fine catch. Many a man'd be proud to have such a comely woman to curl up to in the wee hours.'

'Many a man's already been buried by her. Hear tell she's had five husbands and she's only thirtyfour.'

'All rumors, lad, merely rumors. Don't believe evera-thing you hear.'

'Where there's smoke . . . ' He grinned and pushed away from the counter. 'I'll start loadin' up.'

A sound of hoofbeats came from outside, rattling the shop door. Matt hesitated, a prickle of apprehension going through him for no reason he could pinpoint.

The 'keep shook his red head and smiled. 'I'm tellin' ye, lad, some fella'll snap her up and you'll be left lookin'in. Mark my words.'

'Let's hope they keep the shades drawn, then.' He chuckled and scooped up an armload of grain sacks, hauling them outside and dumping them into the back of the buckboard. Another chuckle escaped his lips. He knew Mr Fuller was mostly joshing him, but he also saw a grain of concern behind the jest. The older man fretted over him sometimes, telling him he saw gnawing pain behind Matt's hazel eyes, a weariness that shouldn't belong to anyone so young. Matt had never confessed what it was, but appreciated the man's friendship.

He straightened, about to go back into the store when he stopped dead in his tracks. A man stood across the street, hat pulled low so Matt couldn't see his features clearly, only that he was swarthy-complexioned and had a smoke jammed between his lips. Wisps of smoke curled into the air, drifting across the street.

That odor.

A peculiar blend for a cigarette, hauntingly familiar. It took him a moment to place it, then he remembered: a Mex tobacco he'd smelled a long time ago, in another life.

A shiver trickled down his spine.

Nooo, please don't shoot — I got a wife and kids!

A shot from the past sounded. He started at the memory, which came all too real. A scene flashed through his mind and he saw a gun drawing level —

No! That was the past. Plenty of fellas came by that Mex tobacco, though he had to admit it was the first he had actually encountered in these parts. Still he had heard it was popular among certain types and he didn't frequent the saloon.

But something about the man's build . . .

You're being downright foolish! he

50

scolded himself, shaking his head. Just a memory, a shadow, that's all it was. The man simply reminded him of —

Rico.

He squinted, trying to get a better look, but couldn't make out anything further about the man. *Rico*. No, it couldn't be. For all he knew Rico was dead. He was just jumping at shadows, seeing ghosts.

A trickle of sweat traced a path down his cheek, cold sweat, and he shivered despite the heat. He didn't like the feeling seeing that man gave him, not one bit, but he reckoned he had to live with it. At least until the day he heard the news the Scarred L Gang had been captured or killed. He shook off the spell and walked back into the store.

The Scotsman eyed him with curiosity. 'Lad, ye look white as a ghostie! Somethin' happen out there?'

'Nothin'!' The answer came too quick, with more force than he'd intended. Damn. He shook his head again and in a milder voice added, 'Just thought I saw someone I used to know.'

'Can't be someone you liked, I'm thinkin'.'

'No, it wasn't. Fact is, if he showed up I reckon there might be more trouble than this town's ever seen.'

A distressed look crossed the 'keep's blue eyes. 'Sounds like trouble we don't want.'

Matt nodded, with a swipe of his hand wiping sweat from his forehead. 'You got that right. Trouble nobody wants.'

The 'keep raised an eyebrow and frowned. 'Comes to twenty-eight dollars even, lad.'

Matt dug into a pocket, pulling out bills. 'I got fifteen to give you now, the rest later.'

'That'll be just fine and dandy, lad. Ye best be gettin' back, now. If I know that brother of yours, he'll be lost without ye. And neither one of them knows how to cook a lick, as they say in these parts. Ye all need a good woman!'

'Like the widow's daughter?'

'A fine lass!'

Matt let out a laugh and left, scooping up the last armload of supplies and with a heel hooking the door shut behind him. He placed the cans into the back of the buckboard and his gaze rose to the other side of the street. The man had vanished. He stared at the empty spot, wondering where the man had gone to.

His gaze travelled farther down the street and he spotted five horses tethered to a hitch rail. This time of morning Hopespring was usually deserted, and the sight of the mounts puzzled him.

Who do they belong to?

He supposed it made no difference to him. He had chores to tend to and worrying about the past wasn't going to get them done.

A knife thunked into one of the grain sacks in the back of the buckboard, jarring him from his thoughts. He froze, began to edge around, seeing a hand, bronzed and leathery, clenching the knife handle. The blade was buried deep into the sack. The hand jerked the blade loose in a downward slice and grain streamed out, piling at his feet.

'Say, *señor*, you might want to get that fixed. You pay good money for that grain.'

A chill washed through his body.

Help me! Don't let him kill me!

Words thundered from his memory and he felt weakness grip his legs. For an instant, he thought he might actually collapse, his worst fears confirmed. But he didn't; he merely stood there as if gripped by some shaman's spell, as past deeds and regrets careened through his mind. Bloodstained images, screams and death. Welling from the depths of his mind, the dark trails of his past. It was back, the menace, the demon. He knew it as surely as he had always known deep inside they would find him, make him pay. He should have killed them all that day, but he had experienced a bellyful of death. He could stand no more and now that proved his undoing.

Coming from the spell, he turned to face the man standing beside the buckboard, a Mexican with dull brown eyes that hinted at a soulless nature. The man smiled, showing brown-stained teeth, and sour breath assailed Matt's nostrils.

'Rico . . . ' Matt said, almost a whisper.

'You ain't carryin' no gun, Señor Brenner. That's not such a good idea. You never know who you might meet in the street.'

Matt swallowed, trying to keep the fear from leaking into his voice. He needed time to think, collect himself. Seeing Rico stunned him, disturbed him deeply, because where Rico was — *No, it can't be.*

'What do you want?' was all he managed to get out. He felt suddenly paralysed by the man's presence, didn't think he could have raised a hand against the bandit had he tried.

Rico smiled and there was something deadly in the expression. 'We want you, Señor Brenner. We want what is rightfully ours. Or have you forgotten that day?' The Mex peered at him with that soulless gaze and Matt wanted to shudder. *Rico*. He recollected Rico with cold dread. The man was merciless, as heartless as any he'd met up with, with the possible exception of the Scarred L Gang's leader, Luther Hinton.

A racking cough sounded behind Matt and he turned to see a gaunt man wearing a too-loose shirt and baggy trousers stepping on to the boardwalk, walking slowly towards him. Another chill. Jetter Braun, the lunger. He was surprised to see Jetter alive. He thought the consumption would have claimed him years ago. Or were these merely ghosts? Had he finally gone loco with guilt?

Once you join my gang, son, you

never leave it. 'Less you get your sorry hide killed.

He recollected Luther Hinton's words to him when he joined up with the Scarred L Gang. But he *had* left, for five haunted years, but never is a long, long time.

The lunger gave him a sarcastic tip of the hat and spat yellowed phlegm speckled with blood to the boardwalk. When Matt turned, two more men stood beside Rico — Jed and Bart Hinton. They were all here, now; they had all come for him, except for Luther.

Rico suddenly gave Matt a shove. 'You got somethin' for us, *señor?*' He pushed Matt again and Matt pressed his back against the side of the buckboard.

'Ain't got nothin' of yours, Rico!' he snapped back, summoning his courage. The shock of seeing them again was wearing off and cold reality was settling in. They were here; they weren't ghosts. They had tracked him down and Luther

Hinton couldn't be far off.

'Beg to differ, boy,' said Jed, taking a step closer. 'You *do* have somethin' of ours an' we want it back.'

Matt met his gaze, eyes narrowing. 'It was never yours to begin with.'

'We steeled it fair and square,' put in Jetter, hacking a mushy cough.

'You go to hell, lunger!' Matt suddenly exploded into motion. He didn't know how these men had found him after all these years, after all the deceptions and false trails he'd laid on his way out of Kansas, but they had, and he would die by their hand if he didn't do something about it. He had no gun, so his fists, which he'd always been skilled with, would have to do.

He lunged at Rico, who was taken by surprise. He swung a looping fist that clacked the Mex square across the jaw. The knife flew from his hand, landing in the dust of the street and the Mex staggered, eyes rolling. He dropped to the boardwalk, shaking his head and trying in vain to regain his feet, falling back each time he tried to stand.

The man named Jetter made a move to get his gun out as Matt spun on him. The lunger coughed a spray of bacilli-and blood-flecked phlegm, giving Matt the instant he needed. He set his weight on one leg and swept his other up in a sideways kick that took the lunger in the breadbasket, propelling him backwards. Jetter went down, crashing into the street like a bag of bones. A cloud of dust billowed around him.

Matt whirled, losing no time, knowing the Hinton brothers would be drawing guns and triggering shots at him. To his surprise, they didn't shoot. They came at Matt, swinging their guns like clubs, but not firing. It suddenly became clear they'd been ordered not to kill him, at least not yet. Luther wanted him alive or he'd be dead by now.

Matt ducked and the first swing sailed over his head. Springing straight up, he threw a vicious uppercut that nearly took off Bart's head. The outlaw staggered a step backwards and collapsed like a dropped tree.

Jed darted in, swinging his Smith & Wesson at Matt's face. Matt jerked back but a glancing blow sent a shower of stars cascading across his vision. The blow glanced from his nose and continued downward, slamming into his shoulder and sending a white-hot arc of pain down to his fingertips.

He staggered, bobbing his head instinctively as Jed regained his balance and set for another blow. Matt sidestepped and the butt whizzed harmlessly past his skull.

Jed let out a curse and Matt snapped three chopping punches that connected with the outlaw's temple, dazing him. He reeled and sprawled against the buckboard, eyes washing vacant.

Rico gained his feet, slightly tipsy, and charged, grabbing Matt from behind, wrapping both arms about Matt's middle. Arms pinned to his sides, Matt snapped his head backward, smashing it into the Mex's face. Blood spurted from Rico's nose in a gout and Matt stamped a bootheel on the man's instep.

Rico let out a bleat and a series of curses, letting go and jumping about on one foot. Matt whirled and buried a fist deep into the Mex's belly. The outlaw doubled, vomit rushing from his mouth and splattering the boardwalk. Matt slammed a knife hand against the back of his skull and Rico dropped.

He spun to see Bart reaching his feet, setting himself for another assault. Matt stepped over, bringing up his knee and slamming it sharply into Bart's jaw. The outlaw's teeth clacked together and he pitched backward, sputtering blood and groaning.

Matt, gasping, lungs burning, started to turn to make sure Jed wouldn't get the chance to mount another attack, but he never completed the move.

Something struck the side of his face and his legs deserted him. He dropped to the boardwalk, dazed, fingers clawing at the dusty boards. He tried to lift his head but a boot toe slammed into his mouth and the world went black.

* * *

Matt wasn't sure how long he'd been out but guessed it wasn't more than a few minutes. He awakened slowly, with a throbbing in his teeth and a humming in his brain. Hazy images whirled before his mind, scenes of terror from the past — that fateful day in a Kansas bank, the deputy — mixing with scenes of the fight outside the general store. A vague worry stirred in his mind: if Mr Fuller had heard the commotion, Matt knew the older man would have grabbed a rifle from beneath the counter and rushed to his aid. That he hadn't mean . . .

The thought startled him into full consciousness.

'Rise and shine, boy,' a voice sounded and a chill swept through him. He recollected that voice, recollected it as if he had just heard it yesterday. The Devil's voice. Luther Hinton's voice.

He opened his eyes, bright sunlight stinging, making his head throb violently. He was in an alley and a man stood before him, a demon of a man, a ghost of the past: Luther Hinton. The leader of the Scarred L Gang. Stringy black hair straggling out from beneath the brim of a battered hat, hideous white scar snaking from forehead to eye. He hadn't changed in five years, unless it was to somehow look meaner, less human than a man possibly could. Matt's gaze settled momentarily on the tooled holster emblazoned with a dragon, a symbol of the power a single man carried over life and death.

'You got loyal friends, boy. Nice to have friends.' A sly smile touched Luther's lips.

'What do you mean?' Matt's voice came raspy, strained. He tried to move but realized two men were holding his arms, Jed and Bart Hinton. To one side stood Rico, glaring, his face a bloody mess; to the other, the lunger, who was half doubled over, coughing a fit.

Luther's eyes narrowed. 'Why, that shopkeep. Came chargin' outa the store like he was lit on fire or somethin'. Hell of a thing. Not many a man got balls like that. No sirree.'

The sinking dread in Matt's belly hit home, tears suddenly welling in his eyes. 'Nooo . . . ' he mouthed, shaking his head in mute protest.

Luther chuckled and licked his chapped lips. 'Reckon someone'll be wonderin' where he got off to. Won't find his body for a spell, though it'll start to stink 'fore long.'

'You *sonofabitch*!' Matt shouted, struggling to break free.

Luther appeared unperturbed. 'I heard that 'bout me. Rumor, I figure. Consider myself a right amiable sort, don't you, boys?' He glanced at his men, who quickly nodded in the affirmative.

'You got somethin' I want, boy, somethin' you took from me.'

'Don't have a goddamned thing of yours!' Matt gave him a defiant look, determined if he were going to die it would be with dignity. He wouldn't give the outlaw the satisfaction of seeing him cower.

Hinton gave a slight shake of his head and snide expression crossed his lips. 'You got it, least you had it.' He backhanded Matt, splitting his lip and rattling his teeth. Matt felt his head spin, felt blood trickle over his chin.

'Tell me, boy, 'fore I lose my temper.'

'You go to hell, Luther. I ain't tellin' you nothin'! What I took wasn't worth nothin' to you, but it's worth a lot to someone else you hurt.'

Luther cursed, grabbing Matt's shirt and jerking him close. 'That ain't the point, boy. No one gets the upper hand on me. No one! *Comprende*? I cain't just let somethin' like that go. Just ain't in my nature. I told you that day I'd find you. I always keep my word.'

'Well, you found me, but you ain't

65

gettin' a goddamned thing! You're wastin' your time tryin'.'

Luther laughed, a sound that held no humor. 'I'll get it. If you don't have it, I want the money that came from it. 'Course I could just rob the bank if you sold it, but that would be too easy. See, I got me a hankerin' to get even with you, boy. And that ain't somethin' I'm fixin' to do quick.'

Luther motioned to his brothers and they jerked up Matt's head. Luther's face lost all expression and he sent a fist into Matt's face. The blow shook Matt's entire body, but Luther had delivered it with just enough force so Matt wouldn't know the mercy of unconsciousness. The men laughed and Luther buried a fist in Matt's belly. Air exploded from his lungs and he doubled over, groaning, wanting to retch. Luther jerked a knee up into Matt's chest and a splintering pain stabbed his ribs. He couldn't tell if one was cracked but it sure as hell felt that way.

Matt felt himself hurled forward by Jed and Bart. As he stumbled ahead by pure momentum, legs threatening to buckle, Rico stepped in and slammed a fist into his face, snapping Matt's head back. His vision snapped clear just in time to see the lunger swing a bony fist. The blow caught him on the side of the head. He crumbled to his knees, blood streaming from his mouth, but it afforded him no respite.

Bart and Jed came up behind him, hauling him to his feet, and sent him hurtling into a building wall. He slammed into it hard, rebounding, taking a double step backward. Luther threw a haymaker that was pulled just enough to spin Matt half around and send him to the ground, but leave him half-conscious. He lay flat on his back, staring up into blurry bright sunlight. He swallowed, blood and spit, head hammering and chest aching. He saw the fuzzy features of Luther Hinton peering down at him.

'You ain't got much time, boy.'

Luther spat at his chest. 'You best get my property or the money from it 'fore I come for you again. You ain't good enough to play my game, remember that. I found you this time and I'll find you again. See to it you have what I want and maybe I'll consider the debt paid.'

Matt tried to focus on the leader, but his vision deserted him.

'You ain't never considered no debt paid, Luther,' he said between gasps.

A sneer turned the outlaw's lips. 'Reckon you know me too well, boy. But see, a few weeks 'fore I found you I found me a friend at a bank in Wichita. 'Course he didn't rightly wanna be my friend, but I persuaded him. Seems you been doin' some donatin' to a woman who lives there. Purty little thing, she is, got herself a passel kids who was left fatherless 'bout five years back and the name struck me as familiar. Now you might not think I can hurt you with much after today, short of killin ya — '

'What do you mean by that?' Matt screamed suddenly, pushing himself to his hands and knees. He struggled to his feet, charging at the outlaw leader, who swung him sideways against the wall and pinned him there, cheek pressed against board.

'Reckon you'll find out soon enough, boy. See, I want you to pay me what's mine, but that ain't enough. I want you to suffer and suffer you will till I come back for you. If you don't give me my due I aim to pay that little lady a visit, give her your regards.'

'You got no right — '

'I got all the right I need, boy. You may not give a damn 'bout yourself after today but you give a damn 'bout her and that's how I'll get what I want.'

Luther spun Matt around and slammed a fist into his belly. As Matt doubled over, another fist clouted him in the back of the head and he went down, this time for good. He lay

69

groaning in the dust, blood leaking into the ground.

'End of the week, boy, that's all you got. I want my due from the one who took it. If I don't get it by then . . . '

Matt tried to raise his head, but failed. He saw boots brush past him, one, the lunger's, stopping to kick him in the ribs on the way by.

An eerie silence filled the alley. He heard the thrumming in his brain, scattered sounds filtering in from the street. He felt the throbbing agony in his skull and in his ribs. He wondered if he were dying.

Stray thoughts flittered across his mind and he saw Mr Fuller, the woman in Kansas, John and Tim, then the gang. Deep sorrow and remorse, fear, took him but only in spurts as his mind slipped in and out of consciousness. He struggled to hold on, unsure why. It would be so easy to just let the darkness take him, release him temporarily from the pain. But John, he had to warn John . . .

He struggled to push himself up, coughing a spray of blood that sent welts of agony through his ribs. Too weak, he collapsed, legs and arms refusing to work right, and rolled on to his back. Head reeling, senses fleeing, he stared up into the sunlight and a vision suddenly appeared before his gaze. An angel, an angel with dark skin and liquid brown eyes, holding a laundry basket. A strange thing for an angel to be holding but right now he didn't have the mind to dwell on it, and it no longer mattered because the vision dissolved as black clouds moved across his mind.

3

You never should have brought him here, child, Althea Williams scolded herself, as she wrung out the cloth into the porcelain basin. The basin rested on a small table beside the sofa, on which she had laid the man she'd found unconscious in the alley. He was in a bad way, with many cuts, bruises, scrapes and scuffs, and some ruptured blood vessels that left rosy patches on his skin, but no bones appeared broken. She saw no undue swelling, beyond the superficial puffiness of his lips and jaw, a bit under the eyes, and that was a good sign. Perhaps there was internal damage but she could not tell until he awoke. He was a lucky man, this stranger. He should have been in far worse shape after a beating like that. The man was strong and that had saved him, though the

72

thought occurred to her whoever had administered the whupping intended that he should live through it for some reason she couldn't even begin to guess at.

She finished washing up his face and rinsed the cloth, leaving it damp and folding it, then laying it across his forehead.

Nearly an hour had passed since she found him and it had been a task indeed to drag him back to her small place. She was strong, used to hauling those big ol' laundry baskets for the townsfolk, but a full-grown man? Now that put a strain on a body, yes, indeed, it did.

Again the notion she should have left him in the alley crossed her mind. It would have meant less fuss and trouble and trouble wasn't something she rightly needed any more of. She'd had her fill of it in the years after the war, a war supposedly meant to free her. A war fought for some, she reckoned, but not her, because she had been anything but free.

Hush, child! she scolded herself, full lips drawing tight. Her dark eyes took on a pained look as a fleeting thought, the thought of the boy out there all alone, frightened, maybe, invaded her mind. No! She couldn't let herself think on it, not now, maybe not ever. The past was the past and though that's where she had left her soul, she couldn't change the way things were.

Was this man trouble? She asked herself that question for the fourth time since she brought him here. She peered at him as she set a blanket over him, wondering. The man had stirred a few times, muttering in his sleep about something, another man, best she could tell, a man named Luther something-or-other. But that was the extent of it. Delusion, she supposed, and she'd ignored it while cleaning the dirt from his face and bandaging the few deeper cuts that needed time to mend. Now, she wondered if she should dismiss his ramblings so out of hand. When he awoke, he would have to live with some pain for a spell and he would be stiff, that was a certainty. Still, she told herself again, it could have been worse. For as she rounded the back corner, carrying her load of wash, she had stopped upon hearing the commotion, momentarily frightened by the sounds. She recognized the sound of pain being administered. Lord knew she had heard it often enough before coming to Hopespring. Peering around cautiously, taking great care they didn't see her, she had glimpsed those men, hardcases all, she had the notion, throwing the young man to the dust then walking from the alley. She had left her basket in the alley and would have to go back for it soon. God forbid it be dirty again. That would mean a bushel of extra work and she felt bone-weary.

Althea pulled the blanket up to the man's waist and unbuttoned the top few buttons of his shirt, to make him more comfortable. As she pulled back the sides of his shirt, a small gasp escaped her lips, quickly cut short. She saw a mark burned into his chest and it gave her a start as she recollected a time when she had been given such a mark, recollected the searing pain and the silent tears flowing down her face. She pushed the memory aside and studied the scar. A brand of some sort, a crude L-shaped thing that looked as if it had been gouged there by some unskilled hand. She puzzled at why he would carry such a mark. He was not like her; he was no slave. White men didn't bear brands unless they *chose* to.

Althea quickly drew the folds of his shirt over the scar, hiding it. She reckoned it would serve her best if he didn't know she had seen it, at least for the time being.

She peered at the man's face, more confounded by him than before. He stirred, moaned softly. He was handsome, least he was beneath the bruises and scuffs and swelling. His face was strong, had a kind look to it, though there was something . . . something she couldn't read. Pain, maybe, a haunting something that had left its mark on his soul. She judged him to be close to her own age, a shade past thirty, but lines of hardship branched from his eyes and mouth, making him look older.

Was this man a hardcase like the others in the alley? Or was he a victim? While the brand indicated he belonged to an outlaw band — that was the only reason she could think of it being there — he didn't look the type; if he had, she would have left him lying in the alley and gone about her business with nary a regret. Oppression made a body wary and insensitive to the pain of those undeserving of kindness. She despised that trait in herself, cursed the man who had given it to her, but it was there and she was forced to bow to it.

But this man . . . she sensed something about him, a lonesomeness, a lost quality that urged her to take pity, want to help him, nurse him. It reminded her of something within herself, that lost little girl who had reached out so many years ago only to be whipped and taken advantage of. That little girl was still there, locked deep within her and peering out with wanting eyes. She wondered what had made him that way and quickly admonished herself:

You're makin' quite a judgment 'bout a man you don't know, child! You should know better'n to take a risk, now.

Yes, she should have known better. What if he found her? What if this man was a link to him somehow? She could never go back to being a prisoner and likely that man wouldn't give her the chance. He would kill her for what she had done and all it took was one little mistake to provide him with a clue to her whereabouts. Was this man that mistake?

Sweet God in Heaven! She'd let herself slip again, let the past burden her. She couldn't have that, no she couldn't. She had a life to live and frettin' on that sort of thing just wouldn't do a body no good.

She stood, sighing a deep-soul sigh, and went to the window. Peering out, she half-expected those men to come a-visiting. Vague fear stirred within her, as it did for no reason sometimes; it had ever since the war. That fear never went away completely; she reckoned it would never let her be. It just was and she struggled to keep it at a distance, lest it overwhelm her. Fear was a powerful thing, her mama had told her, and it had been used against her so often she wondered why she hadn't become immune to it. At times she swore she had, in the bright daylight, where all the past seemed as if it never happened. But in the dark of the night, in lonely unguarded moments, it came back and she would shiver, recollecting the horrors one man had seen fit to bestow upon her. And a tear, just a single tear, would slip out;

she couldn't help it, she couldn't be strong all the time.

Get ahold of yourself, child! He's no master, that boy!

She turned away from the window and glanced at the young man on her sofa again. Wiping her hands on her apron, she sighed another deep sigh. No, he was not like her master; his face, despite the wreck those men had made out of it, was too kind, too haunted. She felt sorry for him. She knew what beatings were like, knew it to her bones and that's probably what had caused her to take pity on him the most. Maybe she owed it to the good Lord above for the chance he had provided her through the minister's wife, the chance for real freedom, if only she could find . . .

There you go again, child! She drew her hands to her mouth in a silencing gesture, dark eyes staining with sorrow and loss. Freedom was a relative term. Her body was free but her mind never would be, unless the Lord saw fit to bless her in some way she could never imagine.

She went to the sofa and gave the man a final check, seeing he was in a deep sleep, then tucked the blanket about his legs. She reckoned he wouldn't come out of it for a spell and that would give her time to fetch her laundry basket from the alley. When she returned she would fix him up a good meal, help him to regain his strength. Perhaps then he could tell her who he was and why those men had seen fit to beat him so. Perhaps he would tell her about the mysterious scar on his chest. She found herself oddly hopeful he would.

★ ★ ★

The dark clouds were thinning, becoming streaked with slivers of light. But with the light came unwelcome sensations, haunted thoughts. As Matt climbed from unconsciousness, he felt pain. Somewhere. Welts of it, radiating through his face and ribs. Was he dead? Had Luther killed him? He reckoned not, but damn well wished he was.

He became aware of a number of things besides the pain at once: the smell of something cooking, a tantalizing scent of fresh-baked biscuits and various aromas from food that made his belly rumble. Sounds, too. The clanking of pans and a sweet melodic voice, a voice as delicate and soulful as the wind. Singing. A woman singing. It was mournful, desolate, yet darkly hopeful in a way, and he listened intently, realizing it was a slave song of some sort, one he hadn't heard in years, not since the War Between the States had ravaged the union.

Matt lay still, letting himself awaken fully, wishing he could sink mercifully back into the blackness. Everything ached. His jaw and head throbbed like a hammered thumb and a band of pain squeezed his chest and ribs. His legs and arms felt stiff, every joint locked. Keeping his eyes shut against the agony, he swallowed hard, the sour copper taste of blood in his mouth. Nausea pulled at his belly and he breathed as deep as he could, trying to keep from vomiting, and the feeling soon passed.

What had happened to him? The events came in hazy snatches of scenes mixed with something else, something dark — a memory of a horrible nightmarish life he had once lived.

Luther Hinton.

The name rose in his mind and realization crashed in. He remembered everything, now. Hinton had found him somehow, and the outlaw wanted what Matt had taken five years ago. But it was gone and he had given him till the end of the week to come up with the money from it, blood money he used to assuage the guilt.

He groaned, a weight sinking into his soul. The day he prayed never would come had, the day all debts came due.

Slowly, he opened his eyes. The

room was blurry at first, wavering, then started to take shape. Shadows were long and he reckoned he had been out half the day. Dusk. Whispering into the day and soon it would be dark.

Where was he?

He glanced around at the room, not recognizing it. The room was immaculate, everything fastidiously placed, tables and shelves spotless. Delicate doilies adorned tables and frilly curtains embroidered the windows. He saw the porcelain bowl, painted with pink flowers. A woman's touch. Except for the incongruous sight of an old Spencer carbine resting on a wall rack.

On a table, a lantern burned low. As he sat up, he removed the cloth from his forehead. Further surveying the room — a parlor — a vague recollection stirred. Had a woman found him in the alley and brought him here?

The dark angel.

The place had three rooms, this parlor, a bedroom to the left and a kitchen. The sound of gentle singing reached his ears again and he swivelled his head in its direction. He swung his feet off the sofa and the singing stopped. Had the woman heard him?

He tried to stand and immediately his head swam. Lowering himself back on to the sofa he pressed his eyes shut and put his face in his hands, giving himself a minute to steady. With a deep breath, he tried it again, this time successful with a minimum amount of dizziness, which quickly cleared.

'You shouldn't be up so soon, mister,' a voice said, and he turned his head. He stared at her, taken for an instant by her dark beauty. She had eyes the color of the richest saddle leather, eyes full of compassion but touched with sorrow. Her hair, dark with traces of red-brown, highlighted her mahogany-hued face, dipping to her shoulders. She was well-rounded in all the areas a man could appreciate, full of hip and bosom and curves. Her full lips carried a smile as fresh as a Colorado morning. He hadn't seen many a Negress, not in these parts, but no matter the color she was fully the loveliest woman he'd ever laid eyes on. The vague recollection now came to the surface and he suddenly recalled the dark angel he had seen just as he lost consciousness.

'You just gonna stare at me all day, mister, or say somethin'?' She gave him a fragile smile.

He tried an awkward smile that hurt something powerful on his swollen lips. 'Sorry, ma'am. Reckon I'm a mite confused.'

She gave him a wave of her hand. 'Lord, it's no wonder, way you got beat like that!' She came over to him and gently pushed him back on to the sofa, bending close and peering into his eyes. He smelled the scent of some flowery perfume, entirely feminine and enticing, and biscuits on her. 'Look clear 'nough,' she said, straightening. 'You got lucky.'

Matt groaned. 'Not sure I can agree

with you on that.' He shifted, rolling his shoulders slowly, trying to get the kinks out. Every move caused pain at first but after a few moments he began to loosen up.

'I got supper on the table, if you'd care to tell me your name.'

'Matt, Matt Brenner, ma'am.'

'Mine's Althea Williams, Mr Brenner.' She scooped an arm beneath his and helped him to his feet, guiding him into the kitchen, where she lowered him into a chair at a small table. On the table were bowls of biscuits and collards, chitlins and chickpeas, sweet potato pone. A slab of cracklin' bread smelled fresh baked and made his mouth water. Although he was famished, eating proved an arduous process. The cuts on the inside of his cheek stung and his swollen lips ached. Despite the pain, he found his sense of taste fully appreciating and he marvelled at her cooking. 'Course he was used to doing most of the cooking for John and Tim, so he had damn poor standards to compare it to, but it tasted like manna to him.

An hour later, he finished. She had patiently waited for him, folding her cloth with precise edges and laying it on the table beside hcr plate. She excused herself and began clearing away dishes and bowls, cleaning them in the heavy sink with buckets of water she hauled in from the outside pump. She set a pot of Arbuckle's to brewing and the sweet aroma of coffee filled the kitchen. If he didn't hurt so bad and have the pressing matter of Luther Hinton on his mind, he would have sworn he'd died and gone to Heaven.

After pouring him a mug of coffee and setting it on the table before him, Althea finished cleaning up. Pouring herself a cup, she sat in the chair across from him, peering at him with her liquid dark eyes. Suddenly uncomfortable, he felt his insides want to squirm. He'd been around damn few women, even fewer of such beauty, and it made him feel like a schoolboy, awkward and tongue-tied. He averted his eyes and his heart sped up, filling his throat.

'You eat like you never had a home-cooked meal, Mr Brenner.' She gave him a smile that sent a funny shiver down his back. He looked at her again, trying to see behind the smile, because there was something else there, something he couldn't pinpoint, something that reminded him of — what?

Then he knew. Himself. It reminded him of himself. It was the same haunted look he had seen staring back at him from the mirror, that look of being dogged by the past, by a restless ghost.

'No, ma'am, can't remember the last time I did. Just me and my brother and nephew and not a one of us can cook worth a lick.'

'You from Hopespring, Mr Brenner? Don't recollect seein' you around town.'

'Don't come in very often. We got

us a farm on the outskirts. My brother, John, and my nephew, Tim, are there right now. They're probably wonderin' where I got off to, worryin' all to hell — pardon me, ma'am, forgot where I was.'

She laughed, a gentle, pleasing sound. 'Reckon I've heard and said worse, Mr Brenner. Don't you fret about it none.'

'This your place?' He ducked his head at the room.

She shook her head. 'Rent it from the minister's wife. She's been mighty kind to me, fixed me up with a job doin' laundry and I do me some dressmakin', too. Ain't much, but I get by OK, least better'n many of my color since the war.'

Matt felt a stitch in his belly. 'You were a slave?'

Her head bowed, lifted. 'Never knew freedom 'til now, Mr Brenner. Was born into slavery and was twenty-one when it ended in '65.'

'Your parents, they alive?' asked

Matt, thinking of his own.

A deep sorrow darkened her face. 'Reckon I don't know. My pa was sold at auction 'fore I was born and my ma, well, she died of the consumption when I was ten. I still recollect the things she told me, 'bout gettin' by and such, holdin' out hope for freedom, but it seems so long ago.'

'Sorry, ma'am, didn't mean to upset you.'

'Oh, I'm past bein' upset, Mr Brenner. It's just memory like everything else. No need to be sorry.'

She was lying. He saw it in her dark eyes: loneliness, wanton hurt, a mixture of weary emotions. He understood how she felt, for in his own way he had been a slave as well, a slave to the past, to the fear Luther Hinton would hunt him down and exact vengeance.

'And you, Mr Brenner?' she asked, as he took a sip of his coffee, easing the brown liquid past his tender puffy lips.

'Me? What do you mean?'

'Those men who beat you, they weren't no locals. Had the look of hardcases, every last one of them.'

A sinking feeling took him. He couldn't tell her about Hinton; he couldn't tell anyone. 'Couldn't say,' he lied. 'They were too busy hittin' me in the face.' It came out more flippantly than he would have liked and he wondered if she believed him.

Her eyes narrowed and her face hardened. 'You saw them plain enough. Reckon I might have heard one of them call you by name.'

He felt suddenly uncomfortable, having lied to her after she had helped him so, but he had no wish to share the past with her or anyone else. Luther Hinton was his ghost and his fight. 'No, ma'am, reckon it was just a random thing. You never know with that type. Reckon they're just passin' through.' He made little effort to hide the lie in his voice, knowing she would spot it anyway.

She gave him a look that told him she

would have none of his shenanigans. 'I take the notion you're hidin' somethin', Mr Brenner. Could that be it?'

He gave her a steady gaze. 'We're all hidin' somethin', ma'am. Reckon you might be, too.'

She flinched but quickly hid it. 'Now you're avoidin' my question.' Before he could answer she stood and carried her cup to the sink, setting it on the edge. When she turned, she gave him a look that told him she would press him no further on the matter, that she understood his need to keep it to himself. 'You best be gettin' some more rest, Mr Brenner. You took a mighty harsh whuppin' and you still need to recover 'fore you go ridin' back.'

'I should be gettin' out to the farm, they'll miss — '

She held up a hand. 'Hush, child! I'll hear no such talk! You stay on the sofa tonight and ride on out in the mornin'. I took care of your buckboard and horse. They're at the livery, waitin' on you, paid for the night. Got your supplies in the back, but your grain sacks were all cut. Reckon those men done that . . . ' She eyed him, smiled, and he knew she could read the answer in his eyes.

'Folks might talk, ma'am, me spendin' the night in a lady's home.' He wondered why the idea pleased him and could hardly keep the smile off his swollen lips.

She gave an easy laugh, waving him off. 'Folks already talk 'bout me, Mr Brenner. I've gotten used to such foolishness. 'Sides, no one saw me bring you here.' She emphasized the last, as if to erase any worry he might have had about Luther Hinton finding him.

'You've been mighty kind to me, ma'am. Reckon I owe you a-plenty.'

'You owe me nothing, Mr Brenner. Minister's wife done me some good turns. I'm just repayin' them.'

'Wish you'd call me Matt,' he said, going into the parlor.

'Perhaps I will, Mr Brenner. Someday.' He settled back on the sofa and she turned the lantern light low.

'That work?' He nodded to the Spencer. She glanced at the rifle and a dark look crossed her face.

'It works fine, Mr Brenner, but perhaps my aim should be better.'

'What do you mean?' He pulled the blanket up to his waist and lay back. She didn't answer, merely gave him a thin smile and walked to the bedroom door. Hugging the frame she gazed at him, an odd light glittering in her dark eyes. 'Sleep well, Mr Brenner. And don't dream . . . ' She closed the door, leaving him to wonder what she meant by the remark.

He lay in the semi-darkness, pain receding and a somber mood overtaking him. The day's events tumbled through his mind and settled heavy upon his soul, a burden of memory and lost time, lost chances, death. The Devil had found him, found him where he hoped he never would. He'd been a fool to think he could outrun the likes of Luther Hinton. A fool, indeed. A deep sorrow rose within him as he recollected the leader's words, that Mr Fuller was dead. It was his fault, another guilt to bear. A rush of tears flooded his eyes and he felt them streak down his face. It was the first time he had let himself cry in years. Tomorrow, he would be faced with the task of telling John and Tim; there was no way around it, because they would see it in his eyes, see the haunted look there and know. They would be exposed to danger and they had the right to be warned. Lord knew, he didn't need more blood on his hands. Maybe they could pull stakes, run, leave all they had built behind. Maybe they could. But would that help? Wouldn't Luther just find them wherever they went? Or could they move from place to place for the rest of their lives, until they grew too old or got lucky and some lawman ended Luther's life?

No, running wasn't the answer, not

this time. It hadn't worked before and it wouldn't in the future. He would have to face Hinton, find a way to kill him, exorcize the ghost once and for all. Do what he should have done five years ago.

He cursed himself. Maybe he was a coward after all. Maybe he hadn't killed Luther because he was afraid to.

You're being too hard on yourself.

Yes, he was. He had seen enough death and it disgusted him, the utter waste of it. He had sworn never to be a part of that again.

But now he was older, more cynical, worn, and the years had furnished him with an understanding that some men deserved to die while some died for idle reasons. Luther deserved death; Mr Fuller did not. It was now clear in Matt's mind, so far removed from that time, and he vowed if he got the chance he would put a bullet in Luther for the old 'keep and another for the deputy.

Nooo, please don't shoot —

God, how the memory haunted him and now he knew why Althea had told him not to dream. She had seen the ghost lurking behind his eyes, seen it and knew it had something to do with what had happened in the alley.

A slight sound brought him from his reverie and he looked up to see her there, standing in the bedroom doorway, staring at him. She was dressed in a long flowing nightgown and once again she reminded him of a dark angel.

'The ghosts don't die so easy, Mr Brenner.' Her voice came low, comforting. 'We just live with them the best we can.'

He took a stuttering breath. 'Ma'am, I hope you don't ever know the ghosts I know. It's more than any one man should bear.'

She gave him a solemn smile. 'I'm already acquainted with them, have been since I was a child.' She stepped back into her room and gently closed the door.

4

Matt Brenner felt an unexpected sense of sadness well in his heart at leaving Althea Williams the next morning. He awoke early, eager to get back to the farm, knowing John and Tim would be worried about him. Washing his face in the basin of fresh water she had provided, he felt slivers of pain race across his chest. His body ached in every place conceivable, but overall he felt stronger. He could live with the pain.

After towelling off, he searched the house, but Althea was nowhere to be found. He reckoned she had started the day even earlier than he, fetching her loads of laundry and attending to her chores. He would miss her ministrations, as well as their vague but interesting talks. He sensed something deep and lonesome in the black woman, yet hopeful and strong at the same time. He wondered what tribulations and hardships she had suffered to put that haunted, lost look in her eyes. He wanted to see her again, spend more time getting to know her, find what lay beneath the shell of strength she'd built around her feelings.

The sadness within him strengthened and he pinpointed the feeling as loneliness, a loneliness he rarely thought about, hadn't wanted to acknowledge. He had John and Tim, and he had his fear Hinton would find him. That had always been enough, at least that's what he told himself in sleepless hours. But he had no one to really share with, confide in, raise a family with. Perhaps Mr Fuller had been right all along in trying to find him a woman. The old man had known what was missing in Matt's life, and in the short space of a day, Althea Williams had made that point all too clearly and it left him with a disturbing longing.

How can you become attached to anyone, now?

The question sobered him. How could he? Luther Hinton had returned for him and odds were by the end of the week Matt, John and Tim would either have to pull stakes and run — or face the gang. The latter prospect boded ill for Matt and his kin having any chance of a peaceful future, a normal life. What chance did they have against the likes of Hinton and his gang? Last time Matt got the jump on him, catching the outlaw off guard. This time he would not have that luxury.

Could he risk exposing Althea to that? To a future that might not last a week, one fraught with death and danger at every turn? No, it couldn't be right, no matter how much he wanted to be with her. It would be selfish, and he'd damn well had his fill of that when he was young. That's what had gotten him into the mess in the first place: selfishness, mixed with a healthy measure of foolheadedness.

101

He'd already placed enough folks at risk, John, Tim, Mr Fuller. Althea had taken a great enough risk in bringing him to her home, nursing him. He could not repay her with what the likes of Hinton was capable.

So he had to leave and not look back, at least until Hinton was dealt with.

Matt's hand absently drifted to the L seared into his breast and a disgusted expression formed on his lips. He'd considered rebranding himself for a time, disfiguring the hideous thing, but what good would it do? It would mar his flesh all the more and the memory would still be there. This way, as odd as it seemed, it served as a reminder of past sins, mistakes not to be repeated.

He strolled out into the early morning sunlight, closing the door behind him slowly, as if closing it on a future he'd never dared hope for. Forcing the thought aside, he eyed the street suspiciously. They were here, somewhere, but the street looked as if nothing had changed, as if the Devil had never set foot in Hopespring. If not for the scrapes and bruises and pain gripping his body, Matt might have suspected he'd simply had another nightmare, that Luther Hinton and his gang still belonged to the past.

The streets shone with golden light, which shimmered from water troughs and rain barrels, sparkled from windows. A few folks hustled along the boardwalk, but not many at this hour. They were oblivious to the terror Hinton could wreak. Fact was, damn few knew the outlaw by sight; anyone unlucky enough to cross his path quickly found himself at the wrong end of a Smith & Wesson. The gang wore masks in all their robberies and killings, but in a few cases Luther had purposely left a witness, delighting in his infamy, delivering a message to the West that the Scarred L Gang struck swiftly and without mercy and woe to the lawman foolish enough to come after them. They had ravaged the West for years — Matt had lost track of just how many — and some even considered them ghosts, uncatchable, governed by laws outside the realm of man. Rumor had it the Pinkertons had been on their trail for a spell, but Luther had somehow outsmarted even them. He rarely stayed long in one place and proving something against him without witnesses appeared damn near impossible.

Matt took a deep breath and moved in the direction of the livery. Within a half-hour he sat in the seat of his buckboard, clutching the reins. The bay horse looked back at him, as if curious why he hadn't come back yesterday. Matt threw a glance at the supplies in the back of his buggy: most were useless, sacks slit so most of the grain had trickled out, cans punctured by sharp blades, a few boxes missing, including the box of cigars he'd picked out for John's birthday. All could be replaced, but Mr Fuller could not. The memory stung him, raising a great sorrow in his heart. There would be no more friendly chats about the Widow Farlaw and her plumb-ugly daughter, no more fatherly advice and not-so-subtle guidance. Tears welled in his eyes but he forced them back. He would grieve later. Now there was only time for decision and justice.

And vengeance.

He clucked his tongue and snapped the reins, setting the buckboard in motion. Riding through the center of town, his gaze remained sharp, searching. Where would Hinton be at this hour? Likely in bed, but by midday the leader would haunt the local saloon, whooping it up with the boys. That was his habit, and Hinton, though crafty, was a man set in his ways. Good. That would make things easier once Matt hit on a plan. This time the outlaw wouldn't escape: Matt wouldn't let him walk away. He wouldn't make the same mistake twice.

As Matt thought about what the outlaw had done to Mr Fuller and the possibility of seeing Althea again, he grew more determined to end the outlaw's life. Perhaps that would appease some of his guilt as well, the blood-drenched nightmares. He would see to it the outlaw fell, or die trying, the way a man should die.

As he headed on to a winding rutted trail into the wilds of Colorado Territory, around him rose a rugged woodland filled with Engelmann spruce and Douglas fir, lodgepole pine and ponderosa. Somewhere, lark buntings twittered the song of a new day. Colorado was so different from the plains of Kansas, and the magnificence of it never ceased to touch his soul. Fresh and clean, unfettered by the bloodstained images of the past, but, now, maybe blood would soak the soil here as well.

He recollected those old days in Kansas, how foolish he had been then. He was young, didn't know what he wanted, which trail to take. John had tried to persuade him to join the family farm after his parents died of pneumonia, but Matt had been impetuous, starry-eyed and captivated by the pulp novel accounts of the Scarred L Gang — until the day he crossed their path.

He couldn't say for certain what he had been thinking that day, only that he felt angry and resentful at his parents for leaving him, dying on him. He needed something, anything, to take away the pain, the hurt. The books were filled with a distorted look at the West, a perverse promise of adventure and escape and as soon as he was old enough he had run away. Spending nights in one saloon or another, he downed more whiskey than he cared to remember or admit, waking up in the beds of soiled doves who had stolen his money and his innocence. He had stumbled across Hinton in one of those saloons, putting on the elephant after some robbery the gang had pulled. One of his gang had been shot and killed — that's how the law

107

had dubbed them the Scarred L Gang — when they examined the body of the fallen outlaw they discovered Luther's initial burned into his chest. Hinton needed a replacement, someone young, sturdy, malleable, and Matt, with his perverted worship of the outlaw, proved easy prey. Hinton had invited that naive boy back to the outlaw camp.

Memories of that night cut with bitterness and remorse, a curse of naive stupidity. Frosty stars sprinkled the sky and looked down indifferently as a fire blazed and a Bowie knife's blade glowed like evil itself.

'You're gonna be one of us, boy,' Hinton said, scooching by the fire and holding his knife blade into the flames.

Matt stared, vaguely expectant, transfixed by the sight while the rest of the men stood around in knowing silence. Two of them suddenly grabbed him and tore his shirt open. Hinton straightened, knife blade red-hot as the outlaw stepped towards him.

'Once you're part of the Scarred L Gang, boy, you can never leave.'

Matt nodded, unable to speak, and Hinton stepped in close, pressing the blade into Matt's skin. Pain tore through his chest as flesh seared with a sickening stench. The knife sliced deep, guided by Hinton's steady hand, fashioning an L that dribbled blood. The wound eventually scarred over, leaving the mark that forever identified him as a member of the Scarred L Gang.

For days Matt had worn that mutilation like a badge, proud and cocky, but he hadn't been prepared for what followed. The glorified accounts in the papers and books didn't match up to the horrible reality of the gang's deeds. He found himself trapped within a gang of cutthroats, murderers, soulless men who thought nothing of taking a life and felt nothing but hate and disrespect for everything and every one. Blood streamed over brittle brown pages and suddenly Matt understood what John had always tried to tell him: these men were no heroes of the West, they were simply mistakes of humanity, a blight on the righteous and just. In his soul, Matt knew — *knew* he had made a dreadful mistake that would haunt him for the rest of his days.

He watched helplessly as the gang ravaged Kansas, robbing stages and banks, murdering innocent folk and raping women. Each heinous act left him more empty inside, more guilt-ridden, yet, somehow, more determined to find a way out and try to set things right.

Then the day had come . . .

No, please don't shoot — I got a wife and kids!

The memory startled him from his reverie. Beads of sweat trickled down his face and he breathed deeply of the warm air, struggling to calm himself.

Mistakes. The past was riddled with them and now he had to atone for that. He supposed it was only fitting. He couldn't let Luther harm that family any more than he already had. Even if it meant dying.

He felt sure John would agree. He was wiser than Matt by far and over the past five years Matt had come to depend on his unerring judgment. John would know how to approach it, how to meet the challenge and threat. Before Matt had put his reverence in something that didn't exist, a false god, a myth created by careless writers and newspapermen, when he should have trusted his brother. That's one mistake he would not repeat.

Matt forced away his thoughts of the gang and struggled to relax as he rode the trail towards the farmhouse. His mind turned to brighter things — Althea Williams. The woman was something else, and he had her damn near constantly in his mind since last night. He wondered again what secrets she was hiding, but how could he question her about them without revealing his own?

He found himself longing to see her

again and for him that was a new and unsettling feeling. He admired Althea, admired the strength it must have taken for a former slave to start over on her own, build herself a life.

He wondered what the town would say if he courted the Negress. It made no never-mind to him, but Hopespring was small, intolerant and set in their prejudices. The women who had offered their attention to Matt in the past would see it as a slap in the face and hate her — though there were others, like the minister and his wife who abhorred such pettiness and narrow-minded thinking — while many a man would try to draw him into a confrontation or refuse to sell to him and John because of such a union. War sentiments and prejudice still ran deep in some states. For some the blacks would always be less than human, mere property to be bought and sold and used. Matt had never seen the difference in men. Their skins were different but their souls were the same and needs and desires — love, understanding, respect, a peaceful family life — were all simply *human* needs.

A smell pulled him from his thoughts. Woodsy and charred, it drifted above the fresh scents of the woodland and morning. Vague dread rose inside him and he stiffened in the seat. He recognized the odor: something had burned. But what? He saw no evidence of fire —

Vague dread exploded into nascent panic and he snapped the reins, sending the buckboard thudding and jouncing faster along the trail. His heart pounded and sweat beaded on his forehead.

You won't care about your own life . . .

Luther's words echoed in his mind, feeding the panic.

Oh God in Heaven, please don't let it be so —

The trees at trail's edge thinned and the land swelled into rolling farmland; in the distance the white-capped peaks of the Rockies stabbed the sky. A wisp of smoke meandered across the trail. The charred smell came stronger now.

Then he saw what caused the smell and a great rush of emotion swept through him. He sent the buckboard arrowing for the sight, for what had once been his home.

'*Nooo!*' he screamed, drawing to an abrupt halt and leaping from the seat. 'You sonofabitch! You goddamned sonofabitch!'

The farmhouse was a ruin of charred boards and smoldering ash. The barn had been burned to the ground as well, and the corral was empty of horses. He stared in frozen horror as genies of smoke drifted from the cinders and occasional sparks snapped, popped, flared. Now he knew what Luther Hinton had meant when he told him he wouldn't care about his own life after yesterday. He wouldn't care because he had nothing left. *Nothing.* The farm was gone and so were John and Tim and he knew that as surely as he knew then he would kill Luther Hinton if it was his last act on earth.

In that instant, all will drained out of Matt Brenner. He collapsed to his knees, tears streaming from his eyes, sobs racking his body. He put his face in his hands and for endless tortured moments memories of John and Tim flooded his mind — days on the farm, planting crops, joking and laughing about the awful food one of them had cooked for dinner, playing cards, planning the future. It was gone now. All of it. Everything that had been his life.

Gone.

'*Nooo!*' His scream filled the morning, rising into the crystal-blue sky like a dying soul. He balled his fists, shaking them in fury at the heavens. 'You sonofabitch! I'll kill you! I'll kill you!' He screamed it over and over until his throat went raw and he had nothing left inside him.

★ ★ ★

Matt didn't know how long he knelt there, screaming at an uncaring sky and feeling rushes of pain, sorrow, loss. He didn't know and he didn't care. The sun skipped a hand-span across the sky and when at last his vision focused he saw nothing had changed. The farmhouse still lay in ruins and his only family was still gone. He'd never felt so utterly, hopelessly alone, abandoned. Not since his parents died, had anything come remotely close to the emptiness inside him now. But in this there was no blaming some unseen blight; no, there was a focus for the pain, a man, a reason behind death:

Luther Hinton.

With shudders of sorrow and strangling emotion, he set about the grim task of searching the ruins. He got as close to the smoldering debris as possible, but snapping sparks stung his flesh and smoke choked his lungs. More sparks, dying fireflies, swirled up as he kicked at the ashes and shards of charred wood. He found no bodies, no mementos of two lives cut short, and for that he was secretly relieved. He knew they were there, but seeing them would only bring on more of the awful hurt.

For another hour he wandered aimlessly about the property, lost and oddly distracted, slipping in and out of a merciful daze. His senses felt numb, and at times he viewed everything with a peculiar remoteness. Then a river of tears would wash that away and a raging tide of emotion would made him tremble and fall to his knees and pound the ground with his fists.

He ran across few of the horses, the ones he did see frightened, confused. He would ask a friend in town to round them up for him, see to it they were fed and taken care of in exchange for some of the animals. He had nowhere to house them.

He saw ghosts everywhere: John's, Tim's, a deputy he had never known.

And Luther Hinton's.

A slow fire of vengeance flared within

117

him, rising above the sorrow. He had only one reason to live, now, one reason alone: to kill Luther and his gang before they hurt anyone else.

For long moments Matt stared at the wreckage of his home for the past five years. A deep shudder escaped him. He had suddenly forgotten how to live.

He went to the buckboard and climbed into the seat, urging the bay around and starting back in the direction of town. Where would Luther be? The saloon, in all likelihood, but could Matt just walk in there and start shooting? For one thing, he didn't have a gun and for another there would be innocent men there. He wanted no one else caught in the middle. It was his fight and he had to tread carefully, plan each move thoroughly, with none of the brashness of youth.

Confusion took him, but he numbly kept the buckboard rattling onward at an even pace, not knowing where to go or what to do, but knowing he had to do something. He fought off thoughts of storming into the saloon and just blasting away, guaranteeing he'd take out Luther, if not all the gang. He had always been too headstrong, John had told him, too quick-tempered with too little thought. He let out a long breath, hands bleaching as they clutched the reins tighter.

The afternoon waned and another wave of grief washed over him, punctuated with occasional bursts of hot tears, burning sorrow, raging fury. How could he go on without John and Tim? How could he go on alone even if he did kill Luther? What reason would he have to live after his lust for revenge was satisfied? None. Except . . .

Althea.

Her name touched his thoughts, along with the image of her face and suddenly he felt a twinge of comfort where none should have existed. He recollected something else — the Spencer hanging on her wall.

He snapped the reins, urging the horse to go faster. Althea was the only one who'd understand what he'd been through and he found himself wishing he could hold her, let her take some of the pain. And though it was a risk to see her again, he was too selfish not to.

He rode into town and faces turned towards him, as quickly turning away when they saw the haggard haunted look on his face. Half dazed, he guided the buckboard through the street until he reached her homestead. Drawing to a halt, he climbed from the seat, legs weak, shaky. He knocked gently on the front door and got no answer and his hopes plunged. She wasn't home; he almost collapsed at the door until a sound caught his ear, a sound that came like a glowing spirit guiding him through the darkness. A shanty sung as sweetly as he had ever heard. Althea.

He followed the sound, going around to the back and finding her hanging clothes on a line.

'Mr Brenner . . . ' she said in a low voice upon seeing him, a look of surprise and concern crossing her face. She saw what lay behind his gaze, the pain, and he knew she understood in a heartbeat.

He tried to take another step towards her but stumbled, falling against a cottonwood. He struggled for words, but none would come.

She rushed towards him, shoving an arm beneath his and guiding him into the house, where she lowered him on to the sofa. He fell back, exhausted by grief.

'What happened, Mr Brenner? Tell me.' Her voice came firm but her dark eyes were wide and laced with worry.

He leaned forward, putting his face into his hands, tears streaming again. She sat beside him and pulled him into her arms, resting his head against her shoulder while he sobbed.

'It's all right, Mr Brenner. I swear it is. It's all right.'

'They're . . . gone,' was all he managed to say between gasps and sobs. 'They're gone . . . '

'Who? Who's gone, Mr Brenner? Your kinfolk?'

A sob shuddered through him and he couldn't speak for a moment. 'He . . . killed them. He killed them both, burned down my farm. Ain't nothin' left.'

A gasp escaped her lips. 'Who killed them?' She took his face in her hands and looked at him and he saw sympathy in her dark eyes. When he didn't respond her lips drew tight and she whispered a name he thought she couldn't possibly know: 'Luther . . . '

'How . . . did you know? I never told you his name.'

'You mumbled it when I brought you in yesterday, Mr Brenner. Reckoned he was one of those men who beat you.'

He nodded, tears streaming again and with her thumbs she wiped them away, pulling him close, holding him tightly. He had no power or desire to resist.

'Who is he, Mr Brenner? Who is he?'

'He's the Devil, Miss Althea. That's all I can tell you.'

'You can trust me, child. Don't you know that? I know what pain is.'

'I know I can . . . ' But he said nothing further and she pushed him back, laying his head on an arm of the sofa. She went to the bedroom, fetching a pillow and easing it beneath his head.

'In your time, Mr Brenner. In your time.' She brought a basin, filled with fresh water, and swabbed his forehead with a folded cloth.

'When's the last time you ate, Mr Brenner?' She gave him a frown. 'Reckon it hasn't been since last night. You left 'fore I had the chance to fix breakfast.'

'I ain't hungry,' he said with more of an edge than he intended.

She studied him, eyes warm, comforting. 'Then I'll brew some tea, for you. You need somethin' warm in your belly.' She went to the kitchen and he listened to her moving about, going

123

out to fetch water, then the sound of a metal teapot sliding against the castiron stove.

His mind wandered then rage thundered up from his soul. Luther. Yes, Luther. He had to kill him, that would help his pain, wouldn't it? To watch the life trickle out of the outlaw, watch him cower and die. Yes, that would help the pain, that would end it. And if a few innocent folks had to be put at risk, so what? In the end more would be spared.

Use your head, Matt! John would never have advised that.

But John was dead. Matt lived or died by his own decisions, now.

No! He wasn't thinking clearly. His pain was overwhelming his good sense, controlling him. He had to resist it. How? It hurt so goddamn awful.

His gaze lifted to the Spencer on the wall and he rose as if controlled by some malevolent spirit, the spectre of vengeance. Going to it, he eased it from the rack. It felt heavy, so comforting. A panacea. He glanced in the direction of the kitchen, hearing Althea again, busy with something, then back to the rifle. He could almost see the hole it would make in Luther's chest.

A few innocent lives.

He took a step towards the door.

'Mr Brenner!'

He halted, Althea's voice snapping out behind him. He turned slowly, gripping the Spencer with white fingers, and she took a step backward. She saw the white-hot fury burning in his eyes, in his soul, and it frightened her. But then she regained control, as if realizing the anger was not meant for her and that made all the difference.

'What are you doin', Mr Brenner?' Her voice came firm, controlled.

He looked at the Spencer, then at her. 'I'm goin' to make things right, Miss Althea. The only way I know how.'

A few innocent lives.

'You can't bring them back that way, Mr Brenner. Believe me you can't. You'll just get yourself killed and that would be a downright shame.'

His eyes narrowed. 'My life's over, Miss Althea. I knew that today when I found John and Tim gone. Maybe it was over years ago.'

She took a step closer, eyes growing sympathetic, beseeching. 'I used to think that way, Mr Brenner, but I know it ain't true, now. You'll know it too after a spell. The pain won't be so powerful, though it won't go away. You have to go on. We all lose folks we love — ' She stopped, the look in her eyes telling of some dark pain, reluctant to share it. Something inside her seemed to take over, shield her, and he knew plain what it was — fear. The God-awful fear of seeing something taken away from you that you needed, that you loved. He had felt it himself when his parents died and he had felt it this morning. And he saw it in her, now.

He shook his head. 'There's nothing left for me, Miss Althea. Nothing but vengeance. I have no choice.' He turned, throwing open the door and starting out, decision made. The risk to life was worth it — Luther Hinton had to die — now!

'Mr Brenner — Matt!' she yelled after him. 'It ain't — '

That was the last he heard because he closed the door on her words and stormed down the boardwalk.

★ ★ ★

The saloon was just starting to fill. Late-afternoon sun dragged shadows across the streets. Dusk encroached and Matt's mood darkened as he neared the saloon. Luther would be there; he had to be there. If not him, then members of his gang. Someone would spill blood for John and Tim's deaths and Matt's fury would be appeased, if not his pain. He hesitated at the entrance, anger forcing the grief back, steeling him. Five years. Five years of running from ghosts and five years of running from himself. All that would end in a few moments.

A few innocent folks.

Althea's face flashed in his mind and he had another instant of hesitation. Through his rage he felt his feelings for her rise and it damn near stopped him. But not quite.

The batwings squeaked as he pushed through. A heavy Durham smoke hung in the air and the scent of it mingled with cheap perfume and sour whiskey, old vomit. Glasses clinked and a few tinhorns laughed, while men from town and surrounding farms shouted and raised glasses to their lips. There were more folks here than he'd anticipated and it gave him pause. Could he be responsible for more death, no matter how noble the intent?

He saw games of poker and chuck-a-luck and faro being played with vigor, though nothing with serious stakes. Twelve tables were arranged irregularly across the main area and a long solid bar ran the length of the wall to the right. The walls were papered in a red flowery pattern that was wholly ugly, but it made the bargirls, who were deficient of good looks, appear more attractive. He surveyed the girls, knowing if Luther was here they would be his first order of business. It had always been that way. Each new town meant new whores and Luther was one for the ladies.

But Luther wasn't here; that suddenly became evident when he spotted Rico, Bart and Jed, and the lunger sitting around a table, slapping down cards. All had women hanging on their arms except the lunger, who looked in worse shape than when Matt first encountered him and wholly unappealing to anyone with a lick of concern about his health. The fight had taken something out of Jetter and Matt almost smiled at that. Their voices carried to him, salted with cuss words for each other and obscenities directed at the women, who giggled, acting interested and falsely shocked.

He saw the barkeep flash him a surprised look. Matt had only been in here once or twice with John, but never with the fury that blazed from his eyes now. The 'keep appeared about to say something but Matt didn't give him the chance. He moved forward, threading his way through the tables towards the gang. He would make them tell him where Luther was; if they didn't, he'd kill them all and feel damned little remorse about it. In fact, he'd kill them anyway. They were all guilty.

Rico looked up as Matt approached, a startled expression hitting his dark features. 'You got *bolas, señor*, coming in here like this.' His dark eyes settled on the Spencer.

Bart and Jed looked suddenly tense and the table went quiet. The rest of the saloon went silent as well and a few men backed towards the door. The gang stared at him and even the lunger stopped coughing. Bargirls got worried looks on their faces and edged away from the gang, sidling up to the bar at the opposite side of the room.

Matt lifted the Spencer, aiming directly at Rico's head. 'First one of you that moves is a dead man.'

'You can't shoot me, *señor*. You ain't got what it takes. That's why you left, remember?' Rico grinned, a dark expression that made Matt want desperately to pull the trigger and blast it off the outlaw's face. He held back, knowing it would not get him Luther, but it took all he had.

'Where's Luther?' His voice was cold, steady.

Rico's grin widened. 'He'll find you when he's ready.'

Fury boiled in Matt's veins. 'You tell me where he is or by God I swear I'll fill you full of holes.'

Rico's smile faded as the outlaw peered at him. Matt knew the man saw the fury in his eyes, the surety of death, and that had sobered him.

'He's right here, boy.' A voice came from his left and Matt looked over to see the outlaw leader coming down the stairs, a girl on his arm. She scurried away from him, a worried expression hitting her face. Luther came forward slowly, stopping about five feet away.

Their eyes met and Luther's narrowed, the hideous scar wriggling on his brow. His hand edged out slightly, hovering in the vicinity of his dragon-emblazoned holster.

'You killed them, now I'm gonna kill you,' Matt said, lips drawing tight, as he shifted the rifle from Rico to Luther.

'Now, boy, we can talk about this. I'm a reasonable man.' Luther's expression didn't change and his eyes never veered from Matt's. He was trying to put him off guard, knowing there was no way to get to his gun before Matt pulled the trigger.

'You lousy sonofabitch! I'm gonna watch you die slow.' Matt suddenly jerked back the hammer and squeezed the trigger and Luther flinched for one of the few times in his life.

But no shot came.

The hammer clacked hollowly.

Luther let out a laugh and a sudden awful knowledge filled Matt. Though he knew it was useless, he yanked the hammer back and hit the trigger again. The same hollow clack sounded. Now he knew what Althea had been saying as hc left — the rifle wasn't loaded!

'Looks like you just run plumb out of luck, boy.' Luther took a step forward, viciousness in his eyes.

The men vaulted from their chairs, Rico making for him, and he swing the Spencer's butt around, catching the Mex in the face. He stumbled back, blood streaming from his nose. The remaining outlaws converged on him.

Matt got off another swing with the rifle, catching Jed in the side, but Bart hit him in the face with a hammer fist that sent Matt staggering sideways. Pain screeched through his jaw and someone, the lunger, he thought, clouted him in the forehead with a whiskey bottle. The room whirled and for an instant he didn't know where he was.

Things began to clear and he felt blood trickling down the side of his face.

Hands grabbed him, hurling him backward over a table.

Luther!

The outlaw was on him in an instant, hauling him up and sending him backward to crash into the bar. Matt sprawled on to a stool, stunned, unable to resist. His vision cleared enough to see Luther's face just inches from his own. The outlaw slowly drew his gun and aimed it at Matt.

'I figured on lettin' you live a few more days, boy, but you done tried my patience.'

Luther lifted the gun and Matt saw his death. He wasn't afraid, unless it was for the woman in Kansas, the one he knew he had failed for a second time.

The *skritch* of a hammer being

drawn back sounded from his left. His eyes shifted in that direction, as did Luther's.

A man wearing a badge stood near the batwings, levelling a Peacemaker at the outlaw. Beside him was Althea, worry on her dark face.

'You best put that away, mister,' the marshal said, and Luther hesitated a moment, then grinned, lowering the Smith & Wesson into its holster.

'Why surely, Marshal. Never meant him no harm.'

'Didn't look that way to me.' The marshal came closer, eyeing the men, who didn't move. Althea ran to Matt, putting an arm beneath his, steadying him.

'Where'd you find the cuffy, Brenner?' Luther asked. His men laughed. 'Thought they outlawed slavery with the war.' Althea's face went dark, but she said nothing.

'You sonofabitch!' Matt started for him, but Althea held him back. He was too weak to resist.

'What's goin' on here, son?' the marshal asked Matt, keeping a steady eye on Luther.

Luther answered for him. 'Why, this boy came in here with a rifle, Marshal. Said he was gonna kill me.'

The marshal cocked an eyebrow. 'That true, Matt?'

Matt said nothing and the marshal looked to the bartender, who nodded in the affirmative.

'He killed John and Tim, Sam,' said Matt at last.

The marshal's eyes went hard. He looked at Luther, who shrugged.

'Reckon I didn't even know his kin.' The lie was plain, but Luther had an ace up his sleeve, one the marshal would provide with his next question.

'You got proof of that, son?' he asked Matt, who looked pained.

'Don't need proof, Sam. He did it, him and his gang.'

The marshal sighed, looking back to Luther, then to Matt again. ' 'Fraid I do, Matt. You give me somethin' and

136

I'll arrest him, but without it . . . '

'Anything I could give you wouldn't hold up in no court, Sam.' Matt's eyes narrowed. 'He'd just walk away. I can't have that.'

Luther laughed and began to move away. 'Reckon you got no right to bother me further, Marshal.' He flashed Matt a look before turning, a look that said their next meeting would come soon, and he wouldn't forget what had happened today.

The marshal looked at Matt, a grim expression on his face. 'Sorry to hear about John and Tim. They were fine folk.'

Matt nodded. Althea went over and picked up the Spencer, carrying it back to the bar. The barkeep gave her a look.

'We don't allow your kind of woman in here, ma'am,' he said, plainly annoyed by the interruption the fracas had caused. 'You best be on your way — all of you.'

She eyed him, lips hardening, eyes

narrowing. She glanced at the bargirls, who hadn't moved from their end of the bar. 'What kind of woman would that be, mister? Decent woman or colored?'

The 'keep's cheeks reddened. 'Colored or otherwise, just whores.'

She gave a scoffing chuckle and took Matt's arm, guiding him out of the saloon, the marshal a step behind.

5

Althea helped Matt to the sofa and set about attending to his new wounds. She dampened a cloth and dabbed at the cut where the gunbutt had left a gash, then at the swollen lump on his cheek. Though these wounds were less serious, Matt felt like hell all the same.

'What happened out at your place, Matt?' the marshal, who'd been standing silent in front of the window, asked when she had finished.

Matt looked up, eyes haunted, a rush of emotion choking him. 'They burnt the farm to the ground, Sam. John and Tim, they were inside, I'm sure of it.'

'You sure it was that fella in the saloon?'

Matt went silent and Althea peered at him.

The marshal, a burly man with a ruddy complexion and jowly cheeks named Sam Johnson, shifted feet and frowned. 'It'd help me if you told me what you knew, son. Can't do a thing against those men as it stands now. You came after *them*, started the fracas. They had every right to defend themselves.'

A surge of anger took him. 'They got no rights, Sam! They got no rights! They take rights from other folks! They kill and they rob and they goddamn get away with it!'

The marshal's eyes narrowed and he took a step closer. 'Who are they, Matt? Tell me that much at least. Tell me so I can get something on them.'

Matt closed his eyes and bit his lip. Opening them again, he gave the marshal a defeated look. 'They're nobody, Sam, and there's nothing you can do.'

'I can't if you won't let me.'

Matt put his face in his hands, feeling utterly drained, and silence fell

140

heavy in the room. When he looked up his eyes were red, glassy. 'There is something you can do, Sam.'

'Name it, son.'

'They killed Mr Fuller, too.'

The marshal's eyes hardened. 'Aw, Christ. Can you prove that?'

Matt slowly shook his head. 'You find him and maybe the bullet will match Luther's gun.'

'May match a hunnert others, too.'

Matt shrugged. 'John and Tim's bodies . . . ' His voice was almost a whisper.

The marshal nodded. 'I'll see they're taken care of. Have Hurly, the funeral man, tend to it.'

'There's horses, they let them all out. The livery man's a friend. Tell him I'll see to it he gets some prime horse flesh if he rounds them up.'

'Consider it done. I'll have him board them for you, too. They'll be there when you're ready.'

The marshal turned and went to the door, knowing he would get nothing further from Matt. Matt saw the resignation reflected in his eyes. The lawman turned to Althea, eyeing her and saying, 'You take care of him, Miss Althea. He needs somebody and he needs to stay away from those men.'

Matt peered at him. 'Watch your back, Sam. Please. Luther ain't one who likes to back down. He might have it in for you now and I don't want to be responsible for another death.'

The marshal nodded and left, tipping his hat to Althea then closing the door softly behind him.

Althea went to the window, peering out as if lost in thought. Matt watched her for a moment, the bitterness inside him overshadowed by the urge to go to her, hold her. He needed her to comfort him, now; there was no one else who could. He stood and went to her, coming up behind her and laying a hand on her shoulder. She responded at first, then suddenly tensed.

'Please take your hand off me, Mr Brenner. Reckon I don't need no more heartache in my life.'

He slowly withdrew his hand, feeling embarrassed, confused. 'I don't understand.'

She gave a hollow laugh. 'You'll just get your fool head shot off goin' after those men. I know you will. Something inside you won't let you leave them be.'

'They killed my kinfolk,' he said firmly, a touch of hurt and annoyance in his voice.

'They did, and that's reason enough to kill them, but you could go to the marshal and tell him everything you didn't when you had the chance a moment ago, and let him do his job.'

'It's my job! Luther murdered my family!'

She turned, eyes filled with sorrow. 'He's probably killed a lot of folks' families, but all of them ain't chasin' him down. There's more to it, somethin' you're hidin' from me. I reckon that's your right and it's not my business to know if you don't want to tell me, but I got enough loss in my life, Mr Brenner, had enough loved ones taken away from me. Don't need no more.'

He felt a prickle of irritation. 'You're hidin' things, too. I see it in your eyes. It puts us on even ground, I reckon.'

'Does it? I'm willin' to tell you 'bout mine. Would you do the same?' Her dark eyes became probing, steady.

He bowed his head. 'I can't. You'd be in too much danger.'

She laughed and turned back to the window. 'That's funny, Mr Brenner. It truly is. I'm already in danger, more than you could know. It don't matter much if there's more.'

'You're runnin' from somethin'.'

'Aren't we both?'

He went silent, uncomfortable with her intuition. She had read him perfectly and though he suddenly wanted to tell her everything about his life, who he was, what he had done, the haunts he lived with, he knew he couldn't. It would only imperil her more; the incident at the saloon had placed her in enough danger already. Luther could strike at him through her and sooner or later the outlaw would realize that.

'I want to show you something, Matt,' she said softly, when he made no move to answer. He liked the sound of his name on her lips but her voice carried an edge of pain. She slowly undid the first few buttons of her blouse and slipped it down just below her shoulders, holding it tight to her breast. He stared at her back, at the scars lashing from her neck and disappearing beneath the cloth, at the C branded into her dark flesh. She pulled up her blouse and rebuttoned it.

A sinking feeling hit his belly. 'Christamighty . . . ' he muttered.

'I have a brand too, Matt.'

His hand absently went to his chest, touching the spot where the scarred L lay beneath his shirt. 'You saw it?'

She nodded. 'When I tended to you. It's on your chest. Would you like to know about mine?'

'I can't promise I'll tell you the same.'

'I ain't askin' you to.'

He looked at the floor, back to her. 'Yes, I want to know.'

'Told you I was a slave since I was born. Belonged to a master named Carter till the war ended. But I wasn't free even after that. Carter had a son. Dale, was his name. A vicious man, more cruel than the old man ever was. The old man for all his faults treated me well, never beat me. He would have released me after the war, but he died just 'fore it ended and his son took possession of me. Dale Carter was a monster. He beat me, beat me hard and often, till I couldn't even cry. He took it upon himself to put that brand on my back . . . ' She hesitated, voice trembling. 'He wouldn't let me go, wouldn't let me free. He . . . raped me, more than once and told me if I ever left he'd hunt me down till his dyin' day. He was insane, I reckon.

I had seen him torture the plantation animals for no reason other than to watch them suffer. He liked to hurt things, did the same with people, but he couldn't show it 'cept behind closed doors with me. He had a reputation to uphold.'

Matt's face tightened. A seething anger swelled in his soul. 'The lashes?'

'Cathauling. After the war ended, I spat at him, told him I was leaving. Even tried one night. He tried to stop me and I aimed the Spencer at him, pulled the trigger. I missed and right then I knew I couldn't kill him, I could never kill him. He wasn't human and I was a fool to think he was. He tied me to stakes driven into the ground, tied me on my belly . . . ' She took a deep breath, letting it out slowly. 'Then he set a big ol' tomcat on my back, tortured it until it clawed half the flesh from my bones.'

'Godamighty . . . ' he muttered, sickened, at a loss for words. He couldn't imagine the horror she'd lived through, the fear she must have felt. He felt fury burn in his veins for a man he didn't know.

Her eyes glazed with tears that didn't flow. 'There's more, Matt. You wanna hear it?'

'Yes . . . ' he whispered, wanting to hold her, comfort her, but afraid to.

'I became pregnant . . . with his child.' She shuddered, and turned to him, eyes pleading, stained with hurt. 'I named him October, after my father and the month he was born.' Her voice broke and a tear slipped down her face.

'Where . . . is he?' Matt asked, emotion clutching in his throat.

'He . . . he took him, sent him away. Wouldn't do to have no mulatto child at the Carter plantation. Wouldn't do at all. There was nothin' left for me after that.' Her lips quivered.

'How did you get away?'

She closed her eyes, drawing a deep breath, opened them again. 'It was one night, late. He was drunk, too drunk to chase after me. I grabbed the Spencer and one of the horses, and I ran.'

'Did he follow?'

'Sure he tried when he sobered up. He said he'd never let me go, even if it meant killing me. His reputation was powerful important to him and he couldn't have the scandal of a black slave on his hands eight years after the war ended.'

'Your son?'

The pain in her eyes deepened. 'I searched for him, searched everywhere but I didn't know where Carter had sent him and no one would help me. He'd be eight, now. His birthday's soon . . . ' Tears ran freely down her face now and she shuddered with emotion. He drew her into his arms and she made no move to pull away. He held her while she sobbed, letting out hurt and fear bottled up for the past two years.

She looked up at him. 'I've been runnin' ever since, Matt. I know one day I'll wake up and he'll be there, waitin' to take me back or kill me. I still miss my son so. I didn't want to live after I lost him but I have to, you see. I have to in case there's ever a chance I'll find him. But I don't know where to look anymore. When I came here I had nothin' but the minister's wife, she took pity on me, gave me a job, a place to live. She gave me a chance and I was determined to make the best of it. But sometimes I don't know how to live, not without him. Not with the fear.'

Matt knew. Lord, he knew. He had lived with the fear of Luther finding him for five years and now it had come true. Would her fear find her as well? Or would it simply destroy her? They were much alike; he realized that now more than ever. That's why she had pegged him so well. She had seen the hurt and fear inside him because it lived inside her as well.

He held her sobbing in his arms, as

the world outside darkened and light bled from the room. They were both so alone, but for the first time in years they had somcone to be alone with.

6

Dale Carter reined up and surveyed the territory. His eyes, set slightly too far apart and slate-blue, filled with disdain as they took in the surroundings — the lush trees and uneven terrain, the distant mountains. He'd never been to Colorado Territory before, and he had no real desire to be here now. He preferred the rich splendor of Missouri, with its southern belles and springtime flowers, its lofty plantations and elite culture. Colorado was for barbarians, that was plain to see. But she was here, somewhere, in a town called Hopespring.

He laughed a razor-edged laugh at the name. Hopespring. Not for her. No, she would have no hope at all when he found her and ended a dilemma he'd been forced to wrestle with for the past two years. She had slipped away from him, defied him, the arrogant whore, and he could never let that go unpunished. Never.

Dale Carter was a wiry man with blond hair cropped close and a wide forehead. A hardness shone in his eyes, a meanness some folks called it, but he preferred the word firm, or decisive. He maintained an iron-fisted control over his life and the lives of others, if necessary. That gave him power, honor, respect; he'd never much taken to that weakwilled compassion his father had shown the slaves, shown all people for that matter. Such sentimentality merely amounted to lost opportunities and squandered chances. He wouldn't tolerate such foolishness. No sir. And he wouldn't have the threat she posed to his reputation and stature among the elite hanging over his head any longer. It was time to answer for her insubordination, her impudence.

Dale Carter was considered handsome in a sort of dandyish way that attracted the fine ladies of Springfield.

He moved in all the right circles, though there were things he carefully concealed from his peers, glitches in his personality most highbrows simply could not comprehend or tolerate. He considered them tools, these traits, and would stand for no compromise where others were concerned. He expected the most from himself and would settle for nothing less from those around him. Once crossed he would see to it the offender answered for his — or her — trespass, but it had to be handled deftly, the perpetrator isolated, the punishment severe and final. When questions arose, he charmed and swayed with his glib talk and meticulously honed manners.

Althea had called it a sickness once and he had beat her for such blasphemy. A sickness, indeed! It was no such thing. It was simply an asset, a progressive entity that guided him, molded him. He supposed he had loved the cuffy in some odd way and she never realized all he had done had been for her benefit as well as his. What chance would she have had on her own, in the 'free' world of the postwar years? He had rescued her from that uncertainty, provided for her, removed the fear of an inconstant future. He was her savior and she appreciated it not one bit. When she had become with child he had seen to it the abomination was spirited away secretly, through contacts whose silence could be easily bought. That had been for her benefit as well. She was no mother, no sort to raise a mixed child. The world had too many mulattos from too many masters' indiscretions already. But she had refused to believe he'd only had her welfare in mind, the ungrateful wench. A child would have only weakened her, caused her more toil and eroded her dark beauty. She had never appreciated the things he did for her, never understood. The beatings, the punishments, all that had served to make her a better woman, tame her wild Negro ways. Those coloreds were all animals to an extent, animals who needed to be tamed. Another favor she'd seen fit to ignore. He should have been a god in her eyes.

Instead she repaid his kindness by running off on him in the middle of the night, by trying to kill him. Ungrateful wench, indeed! His only saving grace was that no one knew she was living at the plantation, except for a few servants, who would never tell. The only servant to disagree with Carter's wisdom had 'moved on'. At least that's what he told the rest of the help, though he subtly let it be known a fresh grave could be found near the river.

No, no one in Springfield knew Dale Carter owned a slave or that he lay with her, but Althea would tell, trying to get back at him, and no southern gentleman could abide with having his fine name disgraced. So he had vowed to find her, remedy the situation. It had taken two years, two years of hired detectives struggling to retrace the steps she had taken after deserting him that night. She had tried to find her son, that much he discovered quickly, but after that . . . Scattered reports nearly pinned her down a number of times and he had raced to intercept her, only to be caught a step behind.

Always a step behind.

Then she seemed to disappear off the face of the earth and for a short time he carried the glimmer of hope she had met with some misfortune. It was possible, he told himself, a woman alone, heading west. A black woman. That made it all the more likely. They still had savages out here, didn't they?

But, no. That hadn't been the case and somehow he had always known as much.

Then came a chance encounter with a friend of his — the only man he trusted enough take into his confidence about the slave — travelling west to the coast. The friend had stopped over in Hopespring for a day or two and spotted her carrying laundry. Once a slave always a slave, he guessed. The friend had wired him immediately and it took him only a few days to attend to matters at home and arrange for his departure. It irked him he had to make the trip alone, on horseback. It wasn't his style but he had little choice. When he found her he would take her one more time then kill her, and for that he could afford no witnesses.

Dale Carter heeled his horse into a trot, a glassy laugh trailing from his lips. Another day, possibly two; that's all it would take. Another day and Althea Williams would learn what he had always told her: she could never leave him, never run far enough or fast enough to escape.

Never outrun death.

* * *

Matt spent most of the morning helping Althea with her laundry chores. She remained sullen most of the time, though he had reassured her he would do nothing foolish. He owed her that much, for what she had told him. The time would come to face Luther again, kill him, but not for the moment. She needed him now and that was something he wasn't used to. Throughout the night, he had pondered her story a number of times, finding himself growing more and more enraged at a man he didn't know, a man who had mistreated her, tried to possess her. He wanted to put a bullet in Dale Carter as well as Luther Hinton; both men were cut from the same cloth, both controlled others' destinies, showing neither compassion nor mercy. Both deserved to die.

With great sorrow he knew how it must have been for her, losing her son, a part of her; he recollected the way he felt when he'd lost his parents, the way he felt when he'd discovered John and Tim had been murdered. Tim had been almost a son to him. Nothing could replace that loss, appease the emptiness. But maybe he could help her in some small way. He knew someone in Kansas who might be able to help. The man had been a friend of John's, a detective for the Pinkertons. Matt intended to wire him before tending to another matter.

The morning passed quickly. He loaded her baskets in the back of the buckboard so she wouldn't have to carry them the way she normally did and gave her the reins, telling her he wasn't feeling well because of his injuries and staying behind. She hadn't believed him and he had seen anger and worry in her eyes, but she'd gone about her business, knowing she could do nothing about it.

Matt stepped out into the afternoon sunlight, gaze scanning the street for any sign of Luther or his men. He wondered what the leader's next move would be. He had seen Althea now and that might place her in danger, the marshal as well, for having made Luther back down. Luther didn't know where she lived but it would be simple enough for one of his men to spot her in the buckboard going about her duties and follow her back.

The thought made him edgy and he'd chewed on it most of the morning. That's when he'd reached his decision: after he sent his telegram he would go to the gunsmith, a man he knew from the times John and he had bought rifles from him. He couldn't pay but perhaps something could be arranged. The gun would serve a dual purpose — to protect Althea and kill Luther Hinton. There would be no more empty chambers.

He strolled along the boardwalk, keeping a wary eye out for any sign of the outlaw or his men. He saw no sign of them. They were likely all in the saloon, drinking or entertaining whores. He stepped into the telegraph office and the operator looked up at him, adjusting his visor.

'Matt,' the man said, with a finger pushing his spectacles up.

Matt took his hat in his hand. 'Need

a favor, Jeb. One I can't pay for at the moment.'

The operator waved a hand. 'No need to, son. I heard what happened and I'll help anyway I can.'

'Much obliged. Need a wire to a man I know in Kansas, name of Clayton Miller. Does some work for the Pinkertons sometimes.' Matt took a piece of paper and scribbled the specifics.

'What's your message?' the smallish man said, poising his hand above the key.

'Need him to check on some foundling homes in the Springfield, Missouri area. Lookin' for a child about eight years old by the name of October Williams or possibly Carter. Check the other agencies and halfway houses, too. A mulatto child.'

The operator began tapping out the message, key clacking in a blur. After he finished he looked up. 'Done, Matt. No charge.'

Matt set his hat on his head and

162

gave a thin smile, thanking the man.

Outside he paused, hoping something came of the enquiry, though he wouldn't tell Althea unless a positive answer turned up. He didn't want her disappointed any more than she had been already.

He crossed the street, a flaccid breeze stirring dust and dried manure; some settled on to his boots and trousers. on any other day he might have paused to appreciate the warmth, the gentle breeze, but until Luther met justice he could appreciate nothing.

He reached Smith's gunshop and entered. Smith, a heavyset man in his mid-forties, eyed him, a sorrowful look crossing his features.

'Heard 'bout John and Tim and the farm,' he said, voice low and sympathetic. 'Right sorry to hear it, Matt, yes I am. They was fine folk.'

Matt nodded, emotion choking him. 'I need a favor, Jim.'

'Just ask. Your money's no good here.'

'I want a Peacemaker, best you got. I'll see to it the favor's returned somehow.'

Smith eyed him, frowning. 'Got a feelin' you might not live up to that promise, Matt. I heard 'bout the tussle at the saloon.'

'A misunderstanding,' Matt said simply.

Smith didn't believe him; it was plain from the look on his face, but the look also said he understood and would let it go. He went to the back and selected Colt's best, setting it on the counter then fishing a box of .45 caliber bullets from the shelf and a tooled holster from a rack. He came around the front as Matt looked them over.

'Tie the holster to your thigh with that thong,' Smith instructed. 'This gun's already got a hair trigger so watch your finger, it's mighty sensitive. Sight's been filed so it won't snag.'

Matt smiled, but there was no warmth or humor in the expression. The gun was just what he wanted. He buckled on the gunbelt and with the thong secured the holster to his thigh, then loaded the Peacemaker and slid it in and out of the holster a few times. He was no expert when it came to guns, but he knew how to shoot. Funny, Luther had seen to it he learned that when he joined the gang.

'Much obliged, Jim,' he said as he headed for the door.

'Hope to be secin' you again, Matt, I really do.'

He stepped out into the afternoon sunlight, feeling the heaviness at his hip and the weight on his soul. He could protect Althea, now, and he could deliver what Luther needed.

As Matt stepped out on to the boardwalk he stopped short. Just walking on to the boardwalk from the opposite direction was the lunger, Jetter. A coldness rippled down Matt's spine and his hand froze at his side. His hazel eyes narrowed, met the bloodshot cloudy gaze of Jetter, who shuddered with a mushy cough and took another step towards him.

'Reckon I could do the boss a favor, Brenner,' Jetter said in a liquidy voice. He looked ten times worse than he had the day before, and Matt took a measure of satisfaction knowing he had contributed to that.

'You should try . . . ' Matt wanted the man to go for his gun. Jetter gave him a curious look, one that said he couldn't quite be sure of the intent behind Matt's words. Jetter hadn't expected to encounter Matt this soon, hadn't expected the defiance in his eyes.

A moment of hesitation. Then a sudden knowing look drifted into the lunger's eyes and with it a dull fear. He knew if he didn't draw first, Matt would shoot him where he stood.

'Christ — ' muttered Jetter, and his bony hand slapped for the Smith & Wesson at his hip.

A cold smile turned Matt's lips and his hand blurred into motion.

Even so, Matt miscalculated the

lunger's speed. The outlaw looked frail, sickly, at death's door, but he still carried lightning in his draw. His hand clamped about the gungrip, snapping the weapon from the holster just as Matt's fingers touched the butt of his own gun.

Jetter's gun came level. In a second Matt would be dead if Jetter's aim matched his speed and Matt knew it would. Matt felt all time stop, hand still in motion, Peacemaker clearing leather, but not fast enough. He hadn't expected a meeting so soon either, hadn't brought his speed up to par. Now he would die for it.

A scream!

A woman's scream.

Matt's gaze didn't waver but Jetter's did, skipping towards the source of the scream a few paces to his right. In that instant, Matt made up for any deficit he might have had in speed. He jerked the gun from its holster, brought it level, barely aiming. He feathered the trigger.

A shot thundered and the lunger jolted, a hole gaping in his bony chest. Jetter stood there a moment, looking up with rheumy eyes, face slapped with shock, at the man who had just punched his ticket. He didn't seem to believe it, tried to bring his gun up, but his fingers faltered. The weapon dropped to the boardwalk. His body followed a heartbeat later. He lay still, rattling cough silenced forever and Matt felt little of the satisfaction he thought he would. It was the second time in his life he'd shot a man and though justified this time the feeling made him sick.

He glanced at the Peacemaker in his hand then lifted his gaze to see Althea sitting in the buckboard seat, horror on her face. She had been the one who screamed, distracting Jetter when she realized the lunger would pull the trigger before Matt. She had saved his life.

She climbed from the seat and ran to him, falling into his arms as he slipped his gun back into its holster.

A door flew open across the street and the marshal stepped out, grim-faced. He strode towards them with purpose, kneeling to examine Jetter. From the saloon, Luther Hinton stepped into the daylight, followed by Rico.

'Matt . . . ?' said the marshal in a sombre voice, looking up at him.

'Was self-defence, Marshal,' said Althea, turning to him. 'I saw it. That man drew on him.'

The marshal nodded. Scratching his head, he straightened and came over to them. 'Figured as much. What I would have said, anyway.'

Luther Hinton stepped on to the boardwalk, peering at his fallen man then at the marshal. 'Arrest this man, Marshal,' he demanded with an air of cockiness and Matt felt the urge to shoot him on the spot. He barely managed to restrain himself and Althea squeezed his arm, knowing what he was thinking.

'What the hell for?' asked Marshal Johnson, peering at the hardcase.

'Killed my friend here in cold blood, looks to me. Reckon that's a hangin' offence.'

The marshal shook his head. 'Don't see as how. Your man drew first. I got a witness.'

Luther's horseshoe-colored eyes shifted to Althea and a glint of intent flashed within them. He rubbed his chin, then looked at Matt. 'You win again, boy. Seems you're gettin' awfully lucky. Next time that ain't so likely to happen.'

'You just go 'bout to your business,' said the marshal, eyeing Hinton.

Luther grinned, covering the murderous glint in his eyes. 'Intend to.'

The marshal glanced at the body, then back to the outlaw. 'Want him buried?'

Luther laughed. 'Feed him to the goddamned buzzards for all I care.' He turned and walked away, Rico following. They went back to the saloon.

The marshal's gaze settled on Matt,

serious. 'Get into the buckboard, Matt. Have Althea take you back.' Matt nodded, lips tight. 'I'll be over soon as I get the garbage cleaned up.' He nodded at Jetter.

Matt let Althea guide him towards the buckboard and he climbed into the seat as she took the reins.

'Oh, Matt . . . ' The marshal looked at the Peacemaker at his hip. 'Don't go gunnin' for any of the others. Please. I don't want to be buryin' *you*.'

* * *

From the batwings, Luther peered out at the buckboard as it rumbled past. His gaze flicked briefly to the marshal, who walked towards a building, the funeral man's place, if Hinton recollected right. He wasn't happy. Wasn't happy at all. He'd been bested by that girl and Brenner too many times now to let it go much further. He was tiring of the game, wanted his money and retribution. But he had discovered a

171

new way to make the boy pay for what had happened in the past two days. He had seen the look Matt Brenner gave the cuffy and that pleased him. Pleased him very much, indeed.

He turned to Rico, who looked at him with a puzzled expression.

'Got somethin' on your mind?' Luther's voice carried an ominous edge.

Rico shrugged. 'Just, Jetter was one of us, Señor Hinton. And that boy killed him.'

There was more to it, a subtle questioning of tactics behind the Mex's words, though Rico would never dare say as much. 'Lunger was gonna die soon anyhow. That fight took it outa him. Hell, he shoulda died years ago. Lucky he didn't give us all the consumption. The boy done us a favor.'

Rico remained silent.

Luther's gaze travelled back outside, eyeing the retreating buckboard. 'The girl . . . '

Rico looked at him. 'Best I can figure, she's just some local who helped him out. Does laundry. Seen her carryin' it around.'

'Follow them. Don't get seen, neither. Find out where she lives and, when he leaves her,' — Luther grinned, eyes narrowing, scar wriggling — 'kill her . . . '

7

'I wish to plumb hell you'd tell me what's goin' on, Matt.' Marshal Sam Johnson shook his head and took a sip from his cup of Arbuckle's. He stood in Althea's parlor, lines of worry and frustration creasing his plump features. Matt could see the lawman was plainly put out, blocked in any recourse he might have taken because of Matt's stubborn reluctance to tell him about Luther Hinton. 'It'd make my job easier and maybe save your life.'

'I wish I could, Sam.' Matt let out a heavy sigh. He wanted to tell Sam everything, let it out, but what good would it do? Nothing would be changed. And Hinton was his responsibility. 'But it's my fight. Like you said, I got no proof on 'em and what you can't prove in court you can't hold in a jail or hang. Reckon I'll just have to wait till they move on me.'

Sitting rigid on the sofa, hands folded in her lap, Althea gave Matt a concerned look but said nothing. Matt stood in the middle of the room, arms folded, face drawn. He had killed one of the gang today but there were three more and Luther himself. How long before the leader acted? He would be incensed about losing one of his own, about another slap in the face. He wouldn't let that go. But if Matt told the marshal about his past it might put the lawman in more danger than he was already and there was nothing Johnson could do unless he caught the gang in the act.

The marshal sighed a heavy sigh. 'Have my deputy out searchin' for Fuller's body, Matt. Didn't find nothin' yet, but it'll turn up sooner or later. I intend to compare bullets and see what that brings us.'

Matt's face shaded with worry. 'Be careful, Sam. Luther'll be more dangerous if he thinks you got somethin' on him. He'll as soon bury you. He's got a hair-trigger temper and don't always take pains to think things out.'

The marshal nodded. 'I'll keep that in mind, son. Best watch your own back, though. After today he'll be lookin' to get even.'

'That's what he came for, Sam. Today won't make a hell of a lot of difference.'

The lawman frowned and set his cup on the table. He cast Matt a weary look then peered at Althea. 'See if you can talk some sense into him, Miss Althea. Lord knows he's a bull-headed one.'

She nodded and stood, going to the table and picking up the coffee cup, carrying in to the kitchen. Matt and the marshal stood alone, silence heavy in the room.

The marshal set his hat on his head and went to the door, Matt following. As he opened the door, the lawman turned, eyeing him seriously. 'You change your mind I'll be in my office later today. If you stop by, we'll

176

see what we can do.'

Matt nodded, face grim. 'I'll think on it, Sam, but Luther's my problem.'

'If he's what you say he is, he's everybody's problem.' The marshal stepped out on to the porch, suddenly halting again and turning back to Matt. 'One more thing, son: Miss Althea's a right fine lady. Some folks 'round here, well, they got their notions, you know, wouldn't much cotton to a white man and a Negress spendin' so much time together.'

Matt nodded, wondering what the marshal was getting at. 'You got those notions, Sam?'

He laughed. 'No, I done too much livin' for that. Don't give a damn what most folks think. But I give a damn about her. She deserves the best. Appears she's had a hard life. I'd prefer not to see it get any harder. You watch out for her, son. Don't let anything happen to her. And if you got notions on her, well, then, you couldn't do any finer.'

'I reckon I couldn't, Sam. I reckon I couldn't.'

The marshal tipped his hat and walked off. Matt watched him walk away, wondering whether he should have told him everything about Hinton, about the past, if it would make a difference. He'd grown damn weary of facing it alone, though he knew that was the way it should be. He had started it alone, those years ago, through his own foolheadedness and it had come back to haunt him. Why should he involve others?

But it always did, didn't it? John, Tim, Mr Fuller, that deputy, Althea and Sam. It always involved others no matter how hard he tried to stop it from doing so.

He eased the door shut and turned to see Althea staring at him from the parlor entryway. She gave a thin smile. 'Marshal's a good man, Matt.' Her voice came low. 'Why don't you tell him?'

Matt shrugged. 'Don't see how it

could help.' He stuck to his argument, though he felt it weakening.

'Sometimes it helps not to be alone with your pain. That's why I told you my past.'

He gazed at her, feelings of warmth, desire, need rising within him. He *did* need her, more than he had ever needed anyone. 'I belonged to that gang once, Althea.' A breath caught in his throat and he forced it out. The ghosts had been inside him for too long. 'I was young, foolish, thought they were some kind of heroes, can you believe that? That's what I had read in all the pulp novels and newspapers. The Scarred L Gang, bandits who lived a life of adventure, free of attachments and emotions. I wanted that. I *needed* that, after my parents died. Desperately. Because attachments meant pain. Attachments meant those around you that you loved died without reason, left you alone.'

Her lips drew tight and her eyes softened, turning sympathetic. She came a step farther into the room. 'We all make mistakes, Matt. Some are worse than others. But we manage to go on.'

He gave a humorless laugh. 'Some come back for you, they surely do. Luther has come back for me.'

'You can tell me, Matt. I'll listen and I won't make no judgments.'

She wouldn't and he knew it. And in that moment he realized that he had fallen in love with her and would trust her with his very life. 'Ain't much to tell, really. I got myself joined up with the gang. That's how I got the brand on my chest. Luther put it there, burned it into me with his Bowie knife. All of 'em's got it.' He took a deep breath, letting it out slowly. 'At first it wasn't so bad. They left me at camp with Rico the first couple jobs they pulled. Came back full of money and whiskey, laughin' it up, braggin' as to how they carried it off and no one knew who they were. Then the next time they took me with 'em and

I realized it wasn't no glory. It was bad, plain and simple. Only it was too late. I couldn't leave. Luther don't ever let no one leave.'

'But you did . . . ' Her voice came low, soothing.

'I did, but it took two years and I'm the only one who ever done it. I found a way to wire my brother, John, asked him to meet me secretly. Luther half trusted me by then . . . ' Matt stopped short.

Nooo, please don't shoot — I got a wife and kids!

The memory stormed back in, roaring with gunfire and bastard guilt, rattling him. He struggled to calm himself. 'John . . . he, he met me and brought his gun. I would have got away scot free but one of Luther's men saw me tryin' to sneak out. John had his gun out and I drew mine. Luther was full of himself a little drunk. He didn't bother to draw. He just sat there on a deadfall like the Devil on his throne, grinnin' at me. We made him throw his gun in the stream and I told him I was leavin'.'

'That's why he's come after you now? 'Cause you got the upper hand on him?'

Matt nodded. 'That and the fact that I took somethin' he had. A piece of jewelry he had stolen from some woman on a stage he raped and killed. The damn thing was almost priceless. I sold it on the way here, got me a tidy sum for it from a guy who couldn't be considered much more honest than Luther himself. Luther wants the money from it, but it's more than just that. It's his pride he cares about. I wounded that.'

'You bought the farm with the money from it?' The question carried no judgment, no reproach and he looked her in the eye and shook his head.

'No, John and I built that ourselves. I keep the money in a bank account here in town, never touch it for anything other than its purpose.'

'You've been afraid Luther would find you all this time?'

Matt closed his eyes, slowly opening them again. He felt tears well from the relief of sharing his story with her, but held them back. All the fear, all the bottled emotion of the last five years wanted to burst out, and he had all he could do not to tremble with it. 'Yep, I have. I kept seein' his face in my nightmares, knowing somewhere inside he'd never let me go. I ain't no coward, Althea, but I could swear I felt him breathin' down my back sometimes. It's a terrible feeling.'

Her gaze dropped. 'I know, Matt. Reckon I'll wake up one mornin' and find the same thing myself. He'll be there.'

He went to her and gripped her arms, looking into her eyes. 'Not if I'm here, he won't.'

She gave him a wafer smile. 'You say it so honestly I almost believe you.'

'I mean it, Althea. He comes 'round I'd as soon bury him with the lunger for what he done to you.'

Her smile warmed then the expression

faded. 'There's more to your hurt than just Luther, Matt. I know it. You said that money's got a purpose.'

He nodded, a distant pain stabbing his heart. 'We were robbin' a bank not too far from Wichita. We had masks pulled over our faces so no one was s' posed to get killed, least that's what I deluded myself into thinking. It was early on in my association with Luther. I'd never seen a man killed before. There was a deputy . . . he burst into the bank, aimin' his gun and I turned, scared out of my wits. I jerked the trigger by accident, startled, and the bullet hit him in the shoulder. He dropped his gun and held his arm, the blood running between his fingers. I just stood there, horrified by what I'd done. He would have lived, but that made no difference. I couldn't move. I heard Luther start hollerin' at me to finish him off, but I couldn't. I could never kill a man in cold blood . . . least till today.'

'He drew on you, Matt, I saw it.'

'Don't matter. I would have killed him anyway for what he done to John and Tim and Mr Fuller.' She touched his forearm, her dark eyes consoling.

'You couldn't kill no one in cold blood. I know it, no matter what you say. That's why he would have killed you today.'

'Maybe you're right, but I could kill Luther or Carter. They deserve it. But that deputy . . .'

'You said you hit him in the shoulder . . .'

'I did. But when I didn't go any further, Luther stepped up and levelled his gun on the man. The deputy kept screamin' 'bout a wife and kids and that just annoyed Luther. I could see the terror in that fella's eyes, the look that said he knew he was gonna die and there would be no one to take care of his family. I never forgot that look. I swear I never will. Luther just laughed and shot him in the head. Rico and Jetter had to drag me out of there and put me on my horse. I just kept seein' his face over and over. I still see it.'

'That money . . . ' Her voice was almost a whisper.

He nodded. 'I wire some every third Monday to his family. It was the only way I could think of to make things easier on them. They don't know who it comes from. First time I sent it I told 'em I was a friend of her husband who had promised to see to it they were taken care of should anything happen to him. I told her not to ask questions, just expect the money and use it any way she saw fit. Made sure she couldn't figure where it was comin' from, though I doubt she ever tried.'

'Matt, it wasn't your fault. You didn't kill that man and even if you hadn't accidentally shot him Luther still would have killed him. Even if you hadn't been there. You can't hold yourself responsible for somethin' you had no control over. You can't blame yourself the rest of your life.'

He shook his head. 'But I can, at least till Luther's buried and I can tell her justice has been served. Maybe then I'll be able to face myself.'

'No reason not to now. You've done more than anyone could do and you can't bring that man back, any more than I can change what happened to me. The past is done and over with.'

'Not for me, Althea. Because it's here. Luther's here. Long as he's alive the past will haunt me.'

She lowered her head. 'I feel that way sometimes, when I think about Carter. I know he'll hunt me to the ends of the earth but I try not to think on it too often, I try to go on livin'. I wonder about the child I never got to raise and hope he's being provided for, gettin' a better life than I could have given him. But I know if I let it destroy me then he's won, Matt. He's won and that would be the worst waste of all. Don't let Luther win.'

'Don't see how I can stop him. He won't let it go and he won't stop until he has his fill of toying with me. Then he'll kill me and that will be that.'

'Go to the marshal. Tell him what you told me. Maybe he can help. At least you'll have law on your side.'

'Like the marshal said, I got no proof against him.'

'You have the truth.'

'What good is the truth? It won't protect me against Luther when he comes. It won't put a bullet in him.'

'But it'll give you an ally and between the three of us — '

'No!' he snapped with more force than he intended. He turned away. The sudden dread of loss rose within him. He couldn't put her in harm's way any more than he already had. He couldn't lose her the way he had lost all the others in his life. He turned back to her, peering deep into her eyes. 'I'm . . . sorry, Althea. I truly am. I didn't mean to speak harshly to you but I can't risk your life. Whatever happens you have to promise me you won't lift a hand against Luther again. I've put you in enough danger.'

She gave him a thin smile and he saw her lips tremble. 'I love you, Matt. I think I have since the moment I found you in the alley. Something . . . ' She shook her head. 'Something in your eyes. I've been alone a long time, but I never noticed much 'fore now, till I met you. I put all those feelings away. Didn't have any need for them. You made me think maybe there was more to life than just existin' the way I have been.'

Warmth rose inside him and he knew he had been longing to hear those words all his life. He had known her only a brief time but he didn't think he'd ever loved anyone or anything so completely. 'I feel the same way, Althea. Truly I do. And I couldn't bear the thought of losin' you to him.'

'Shhh,' she whispered, placing her finger to his lips. 'Not tonight. Let's talk no more of it.' Her fingers went to her blouse, slowly undoing the buttons. She slipped it from her shoulders, letting it drop to the floor. He peered at her dark beauty, a feeling he had never known rushing through him, completing him, filling the empty spaces. He took her in his arms, kissing her deeply, hungrily. He let her guide him to her bedroom, powerless to resist, to deny the emotion that swept through him in great warm waves. He wouldn't have wanted to. For the first time he could remember he wasn't alone, and he knew even if Luther killed him tomorrow he never would be again.

★ ★ ★

Rico Valez's dark eyes narrowed as he tried to see into the small dwelling, endeavoring to pick out the shapes of Matt Brenner and the dark woman. They had proved easy to follow, too easy for Rico liked the challenge of tracking and this had given him none. Luther said to kill her as soon as the boy left and that he would, enjoying the very act. But first he would pay her some special attention, let her know what a real man was like. He rather fancied a dark woman; he was damned tired of saloon whores and cheap trollops who smelled like rotgut whiskey and two-bit perfume and old favors. He had hoped the boy would leave tonight and considered killing him just for the hell of it, but decided against it. If he disobeyed Luther's orders he'd never get the chance at another woman again. He'd never get the chance at anything. Men who didn't obey Luther didn't live long.

Rico was surprised the leader had let the boy live as long as he had. That brooch didn't matter a lick to Luther, not really, though he always wanted more money. Rico knew there was much more on the leader's mind: his twisted sense of pride made him want revenge on the boy for getting the better of him five years ago. Rico couldn't understand it. He would have surely killed the boy if he had run across him somewhere, but he never would have gone out of his way for such a thing. Luther was risking too much by letting this go on, toying with the *gringo*. Already one of their own had been killed. *Madre de Dios!* But there was no way to tell Luther that without getting dead, so Rico didn't say a word.

No matter. It would be over soon. As soon as the boy left tomorrow he would pay the girl a visit and kill her. Then there would be nothing more to take from the boy and Luther could finish the job he should have done that first day they hit town.

Rico peered again at the darkened window, anxious and tired of sitting still. He doubled low and scuttled across the street, sneaking up to the window and chancing a look inside. Nothing. He could not see the boy anywhere but he was positive they were both in the house, so that meant they had retired for the night. Rico spat in disgust and grunted, going back to his spot across the street and tucking himself away in an alley where he could watch the house at a good angle. *Madre de Dios*, it was going to be a long night.

8

Marshal Sam Johnson rose with the sun. He peered out through the dust-coated window of his office, scanning a street lit with a fresh sheen of morning gold. How serene Hopespring could look in the morning, before the day took hold and the dust rose. The town might not have had a care in the world. But the gold couldn't cover the tarnish that lay beneath, the tarnish brought by the likes of those men he'd encountered in the saloon yesterday.

He knew Matt Brenner was right about those men. Sam had puzzled over them when they rode into town a couple days ago. He immediately pegged them as hardcases, no doubt about it. But what did they want? That had been his question. He still didn't know completely, but he knew it had something to do with Matt Brenner. He knew they had killed Matt's brothers and were likely planning on some other crime before they left. He knew it like he knew his gout would pain him during the rainy season. Men like that . . . well, they never just left peaceably. But like he told the boy, he needed proof to arrest them and as a lawman he generally went by the letter. Oh, he might stretch it a bit here and there, as he had yesterday by simply accepting Miss Althea's witness to the shooting, knowing full well she would say just about anything short of out-and-out lying to protect the boy. He saw the love she held for Matt in her eyes, even if she refused to realize it herself yet. He had seen the same thing in Matt's and that made him smile. He had known Matt and John a few years now, considered them right decent folk, but knew Matt had always been running from something inside, some ghost. For a time he'd pondered about it, wondering what it was, but soon gave it up, knowing the boy wasn't likely to tell. But it was serious business, whatever it was and likely south of the law; no man looked that haunted unless his hands were stained with blood. It didn't matter to Sam, though. He based his accounting of Matt on the way he had acted since coming to Hopespring, not on some hidden past. For whatever wrong Matt Brenner had committed, the boy had more than paid for it in guilt; that was good enough for Sam Johnson.

That aside, he found himself wishing Matt would tell now because he felt sure it involved those men in the saloon. And just maybe it would provide him with some leverage against the hardcases, give him a chance to prevent whatever they had in mind.

He considered the hardcases, running a finger over his upper lip. He had seen the deadness in their eyes, especially in those of the one called Luther. That man was as cold as the Devil himself, in Sam's estimation, fully capable of doing what Matt accused him of.

But what could he do if Matt didn't come clean?

Not goddamn much. He had shifted through a stack of Wanted dodgers, been up half the night doing it. Surely a man like that would have a price on his hide. But he found nothing. He could only assume the man had used a mask, had never been accurately identified, or killed those who could implicate him.

Sam Johnson went to the rickety wooden table against the left wall and poured himself a cup of Arbuckle's from the metal pot. It was cold and powerful enough to eat the dung out of a horseshoe and he winced as he sipped at it. Nothing like Miss Althea's coffee. That woman had a touch with things, a God-given gift, if he did say so himself. He had told her to make it strong and she sure as hell obliged. 'Course it was yesterday's brew so that probably helped.

He thought about the black woman, shaking his head. A fine woman, but she was an enigma, too. She had come

into town about two years ago with
little more than the clothes on her
back. He had watched her step off
the stage, weary and frightened, but
doing her damnedest not to show it.
She was running from something, just
like Matt; she had that look about her.
But it didn't matter a lick to him
because if little else he was a right
good judge of folk and he could tell
she was one of the best. She was a
victim of some unknown circumstance,
not a participant. But he'd never felt
pity for her because she would have
taken it as an insult and didn't need
it from him or anyone else. She was
a strong woman, a survivor, and all he
could give her was his deepest respect.
That's why he had not questioned
her about the killing yesterday. She
deserved whatever leeway she asked
for and he felt only too happy to
provide it.

All things considered, Matt and
Althea were much alike, he decided.
Much alike. Each was running, hiding,

and each carried on with an indomitable spirit that drove them forward against adversity, made them defy all odds. Each had been battered by life, but each had come through with perseverance, pride and promise. Lesser men — or women — might simply have given in, let their ghosts overwhelm them. He admired them more than he could say and wondered if, things reversed, he would have had the strength to do the same.

But would they come through this time?

He wondered. Those men, they wanted something, and if he reckoned right they wanted Matt to provide it. Althea was in danger, too; he saw that in the leader's eyes yesterday. She had interfered and he wanted to get even but there was more to it than that. The leader saw the same thing in Matt's eyes Sam did: love for her. And love in the hands of such a man was a dangerous weapon.

Sam Johnson went to his desk and

fell into his chair, setting his coffee on the desktop. He rubbed his eyes and let out a long sigh. Glancing at the stack of Wanted dodgers, he debated whether to look through them again. No, it would do no good; he had missed nothing the first time. The thought frustrated him. Something had to be there, somewhere. And he needed to find it fast. With that sixth sense his years as marshal had provided him, he felt the time growing short.

You could try talkin' to the boy again, he told himself, letting out a heavy sigh. Yes, he could try, but he had the notion it would do him little good unless Matt decided to speak on his own. He had held his secrets this long, it would take an act of God to pry them loose.

Or an act of woman.

He ran a hand through his hair. Yes, maybe that was it. He could talk to Miss Althea when the boy wasn't around. If anyone could convince Matt to tell she could. He might listen to her. But would she help? He reckoned she might. He would convince her of what he had seen in the leader's eyes, convince she was in danger, as well as Matt. Sam knew in his heart the outlaw would kill the boy soon, so it would be no lie. And Miss Althea wasn't one to let a kind deed go unreturned. Two years ago, he'd introduced her to the minister's wife, who trusted Sam's judgment in folks as much as her own and had given Althea a job and home. Althea had told him many times she would give him free laundry, had cooked him a few of her magnificent homecooked meals. If he asked her as a favor . . .

It was decided then. He would try it. It was one of his few options.

He saw one other thing he could do. He would wire the authorities in Denver about the man named Luther Hinton. If anything could be proved against the fella they would know. He would try a friend in Houston, too, and stress the need for urgency, tell them it was a matter of life or death — which it was — and by the end of the day he hoped something would turn up, something he could bring to a judge after he arrested the hardcase and his men.

The door rattled open and Sam Johnson, pulled from his thoughts, looked up to see his deputy entering the office. The deputy's face had a haggard look, punctuated by bloodshot eyes. The marshal knew he had been up all night searching for the body of Fergus Fuller, the general store owner.

Marshal Johnson peered at the deputy, who came over to the desk, dropping heavily into a hardbacked chair.

'I shoulda been lookin' a little closer to home, Marshal,' he said, voice strained, face going a shade paler. Sam knew there was more to the deputy's look than simple exhaustion.

'You found him?' Sam straightened in his chair, leaning forward and setting his elbows on the desk.

The deputy nodded, disgust in his eyes. 'Yep. Funny thing is, I figured it'd be hidden somewhere not so obvious, like down by the stream. That's where I focused my search, even got me a few locals to help poke around. But nothing. Seemed as if Mr Fuller just walked off the face of the earth.'

'Where?' The marshal's eyes narrowed. His face went grim.

'Damnedest thing, Marshal. Right there in his own store. They buried him under a bunch of grain sacks and such in the back. Sure did a job on him. Shot him up somethin' awful. Surprised nobody heard it, but looks like they backed him inside and shot him through some sacks to muffle the sound. Smell was somethin' to cause nightmares, too.' The deputy made a face that told the marshal he was having a hard time holding on to his breakfast. Disgust and fury rose within Sam at the utter brutality of it. Mr Fuller was a decent man, kind and generous to a fault sometimes. He'd lived all his life in Hopespring and deserved better.

'Looks like these *hombres* got more brains and balls than I gave them credit for.'

The deputy nodded. 'Reckon so. Might've spent months lookin' for it if I hadn't taken a notion to look around the store again for clues. I got to noticin' that smell and 'fore long I tracked it down. They'd even moved some stock over bloodstains on the floor.'

'They must have figured they be gone by the time anyone found it and without witnesses they'd get away scot free.'

'Figure it that way, too, Marshal.'

'Funeral man take the body?'

'Yep, just like you instructed. Said he'd have a bullet for you a little after noon. There's plenty of them to choose from and I reckon they come from more than one gun.'

'Only one gun I'm worried about, son, and that's the one that belongs to Hinton. I want to match the bullet with his if we have to dig every slug out of Fergus to do it. If it don't match his it'll match one of his men's and as far as I'm concerned that will be enough to arrest 'em all and hang 'em.'

'What you gonna do now?'

The marshal gave him a weary smile. 'Gonna go have me a parley with that fella, son. And gonna get me a bullet.'

* * *

The saloon was virtually deserted at eight in the morning. A couple of leftover patrons, ones whom the 'keep had taken pity on because they'd been too drunk to walk home, slumped over tables, nursing whiskey hangovers and cringing at the least little noise. Saloon girls lazed about, sweeping floors or cleaning glasses with little enthusiasm. A few entertained the men sitting around one table, sitting on their laps and smiling wooden smiles, hoping to get more of what they came by the night before. Luther Hinton was a sonofabitch in the worst sense but he was generous with his women. He went through money like water, chiefly because he figured he had an endless supply of it. There was always a bank around with a bottomless account assigned just to him and his Smith & Wesson.

Luther had risen early today, in fact had never really gone to sleep. He'd entertained Miss Lucy for the better part of the night, or rather she'd entertained him. She sat on his lap, now, a bruise ripening on one eye. She had endeavored to cake make-up over it but it was livid, peeking through. As loose as Luther was with his cash he was with his callous treatment of doves. He had made her do things most bargirls weren't used to doing and she had taken some loosening up to do them. Luther found his fists generally got a lady loosened in right fine fashion. She had taken it and come back for more, richer by far in greenbacks than the rest of the girls, if not in pride.

With a grunt he shoved her away and she gave him a put-out look, jamming her hands to her hips. 'Go on, git!' he snapped. 'There'll be more later. An' get me a whiskey!'

The girl frowned, but after seeing the look in his eyes scurried off and returned shortly with the whiskey, then made herself scarce. Luther nodded to the rest of the men, who disentangled themselves from doves and patiently waited for Luther's next words.

The outlaw leader studied the faces of Bart and Jed Hinton, his brothers, his kin, knowing he'd sacrifice either in an instant if they disobeyed him. He was one lowly cuss, he had to admit, but that rather pleased him.

Luther had been thinking. There was the boy, whom he fully intended on killing not so long after the cuffy died. She was to be his last taunt; let Matt Brenner find the cuffy all done up the way only Rico could. That's why he had sent the Mex, knowing full well Rico would not just kill her. No, the Mex had a way with the ladies, a sadistic way that surpassed even the meanness of Luther himself. He respected that. Wasn't often he ran across someone as talented and rotten as himself. He wished he could be there when Brenner discovered what was left of her, wished he could see the look on the boy's face. He chuckled, finding the whole situation gloriously funny. He'd waited five years for this and soon his vengeance would be complete. No one got the upper hand on Luther Hinton. No one. Not some backwoods farmer boy with a piece of short-lived luck on his side nor some cupid-lipped darkie.

Nor some hick town marshal. Now there was another burr in his saddle. The marshal had manoeuvered a back-down in the saloon the other day and he had let the boy go free after killing Jetter. Luther didn't rightly give a galldamn that the lunger had gotten himself buried but the marshal should have seen his view on things. It would have saved the man a whole lot of grief. He hadn't quite decided how he wanted to kill the lawman, but maybe he'd let Jed handle it. Jed hadn't killed anyone in a spell; he deserved some fun.

Luther had a more immediate problem, however. He usually didn't stay over so long in one town and it had put a drain on his resources. He'd spent *mucho dinero* on that Lucy and he had a certain code of honor about that. He always let the whores keep the money. His mammy had been a bargirl and he respected the trade.

He eyed his brothers again and neither moved, though expectant looks crossed their eyes.

'Looks like we'll be needin' some cash 'fore we finish in this town.' He poked the brim of his hat up and narrowed his eyes. The hideous scar wriggled, repulsive.

'What you got in mind, Luther?' Jed asked.

'Been thinkin' 'bout the bank yonder.' He nodded in the direction of the door. 'Stands to reason that boy ain't gonna tell us what he done with that brooch. Reckon he got the money from it stashed in the bank, so I'll jest have to take it anyhow. Might as well help ourselves to some extra while we're at it.'

'We're with you, Luther, shorely we are,' said Bart. Bart wasn't the smartest of the group; Luther knew it, but he was fiercely loyal and that made up for the lack of brains.

' 'Course you are, Bart, or you'd be buried.' Luther chuckled, breaking the strained silence that followed the remark. Bart and Jed laughed, too. They had no choice.

'When?' asked Bart.

Luther leaned back and spat on the floor. 'Whelp, been noticin' business picks up just 'fore noon. Figure we wait a spell after that, hit 'em next to closin'-time, when they're countin' all the money.'

'We leavin' after that?'

'Yep. Rico ain't reported back yet so I figure he'll get the girl done today. Ain't much after that. We'll make sure the boy gets one last visit with her 'fore we go.' Luther grinned and Jed and Bart let out uneasy chuckles.

'What about the boy, Luther?' Bart swiped the back of his hand across his leaking nose.

Luther looked coldly pensive. 'Been thinkin' 'bout that, too. Thought maybe the girl would be his last chance to suffer but then I got a notion there's one last way to make him pay.'

The brothers glanced at each other, then Luther. 'How's that, Luther?' Jed asked.

'Done me lots of thinkin' after that boy got the jump on us five years back. Took me a spell to pin it down but I reckon he changed after that

211

bank holdup when I killed that deputy. Think that's when he took the notion to get out. After I found out he was sendin' money to the deputy's woman I put two and two together.'

'I don't foller, Luther.' Bart scratched his head and crinkled his brow.

A sneer turned Luther's lips. 'Told the boy once you join the Scarred L Gang you never leave. Boy's gonna accompany us on that bank job, fellas. And after we're gonna leave him dead in the street for everybody to find. Won't be no bigger disgrace to him than that. Figure I can enjoy my revenge even after he's dead.'

Bart and Jed smiled, eyes brightening, and Luther had to admit it was a stroke of genius. His plan for revenge was drawing to completion and he had never felt so pleased with himself in his life. This time nothing would stop him from punching that boy's ticket. Nothing.

* * *

The marshal felt a tingle of nerves in his belly as he made his way across the street towards the saloon. He had to admit it wasn't often he'd been placed in such a situation, facing down a killer. But he had always known the day would come and he would take it like a man. Luther Hinton was about to find out Marshal Sam Johnson was no pushover and he wouldn't stand for the likes of him killing innocent folk in his town.

Fuller's body had been the thing he'd been waiting for. A chance at nailing down proof on the outlaws. He had worried they had hidden it so well it would never be found, despite the fact he had the utmost confidence in his deputy. The woodland around Hopespring was dense and there were a hundred places to hide a body; it might not be found until it was a boneman and that would be no good. He needed those bullets. It was a stroke of luck the deputy had found it so soon and Sam intended to make the most of it.

It was also a risky proposition. Luther Hinton might decide to kill him then and there. He couldn't be sure about the man, but a marshal would be a whole lot more difficult to shoot in plain view than a storekeeper. That's why Sam chose to confront him in the saloon. The 'keep and some of the girls would be there. Luther would be less likely to try anything.

Marshal Johnson stopped just outside the batwings, peering at them, sucking a deep breath. He slid his Peacemaker from its holster, checking its load and making sure all was in order. He slid it in and out of the holster a few times to get a good feel of its motion.

At last he pushed through the doors, and stood just inside, surveying the place, spotting the man and two of his gang sitting at a rear table. He wondered a moment about the missing one, the Mex, but supposed he was still upstairs. He glanced at the barkeep, who gave him a curious look, then at the handful of doves leaning on the bar. He tipped his hat to the 'keep and walked towards Luther's table.

The outlaw looked up, a smug expression on his face and Marshal Johnson had the urge to just fill the bastard with holes right there. Only his sense of decency held him back and that hung by a thread.

'Mornin', Marshal.' Luther smiled an infuriating smile. 'You're startin' your drinkin' mighty early.'

'Didn't come here to drink, Hinton, you know that.'

Luther put on a puzzled look. 'No? Sorry to hear that. I hate drinkin' alone.'

The marshal pulled out a chair and lowered himself into it, forcing his nerves to steady, holding the outlaw's gaze. He cast the other two a quick look, but saw nothing in their eyes. They appeared surprised to see him, a bit confused by it, and he reckoned they didn't do much of the thinking.

'Found us a body this mornin', Hinton,' the marshal said after a moment of pregnant silence.

'That s'posed to mean somethin' to me?'

'Mr Fuller. Owned the general store. Found him 'neath some sacks in the back. He'd been shot up pretty bad.'

'Sorry to hear that, Marshal.' He wasn't sorry at all. His voice told as much. In fact, it was taunting, playful in a perverse way.

'Are you?' The marshal held the outlaw's gaze.

'Why, yes. Mighty sad whenever someone passes, don't you think?' One of the men stifled a laugh and Luther shot him a sharp look. Sam knew he was being toyed with and it irritated him no end. The thought of putting a bullet in the man became all the more appealing.

He came right out with it, having no belly for the outlaw's games. 'You didn't make that body, did you, Hinton?'

'Ain't had me the opportunity to visit the general store, Marshal. Don't know anyone named Fuller.'

He was lying; Sam saw it plain as day. He remained silent a moment, wondering if he had much of a chance rattling a man like Luther Hinton. He decided he didn't; the man was far too practised at this game, far too callous and hardened. It was his bet and he held all the aces. Sam had no chance at a bluff.

'Give me your gun, Hinton,' said the marshal.

Without a word, Jed Hinton began to slip his Smith & Wesson out of its holster beneath the table. Sitting next to him, Luther noticed the movement and gave a slight shake of his head. Jed eased the gun back in.

'What for, Marshal? I ain't done nothin' wrong.' Hinton's gaze didn't waver.

The marshal's hand went to the butt of his Peacemaker, rested there. 'It ain't a request, Hinton. Ease it out of the holster and set it on the table.'

Hinton hesitated, the smile fading

from his lips and something icy crossing his horseshoe-colored eyes. But he complied, sliding the Smith & Wesson out and laying it on the table. The marshal reached over and pulled it to him, lifting it and letting the bullets trickle out on to the table. Gun empty, he passed it back to Hinton.

'What the hell you want with my bullets?' the outlaw asked, all pretence of servility dropping from his face.

'Mr Fuller stopped a bunch of bullets 'fore he died. Reckon one of them might match the ones in your gun.'

Hinton remained silent for a moment. 'You best watch your back, Marshal. I don't like folks questioning my honesty.'

Sam didn't flinch. 'That a threat, Hinton? There's penalties for threatening a lawman.'

Hinton didn't even attempt to bluff. 'I never threaten.'

'See to it you don't.' The marshal held his gaze as he stood, sliding back the chair with a foot. He scooped up the bullets and slid them into a pocket. 'I'm tellin' you straight, Hinton, even if these don't match I want you out of town 'fore the sun comes up tomorrow. I'll know by this afternoon if they do and I'll come get you. You don't hear from me by then, start packing. And stay away from the Brenner boy, you hear?' The marshal backed towards the door, giving the barkeep a last tip of his hat. The 'keep had a strained look on his face; he clearly didn't like his bar being the place for a confrontation.

On the street, the marshal felt little pleased with himself. He had done what he set out to do but it gave him no satisfaction. He would only feel that when Luther Hinton was gone for good, one way or another.

He crossed the street, intending to head on over to the funeral man's to see if the fella had made any progress with the bullets. He was anxious to see if they matched and had the gut feeling they would. But as he stepped on to the boardwalk he stopped. A man sitting atop a horse outside his office caught his attention and he peered at him, wondering. He had never seen the fella before, a dandy-looking dude with blond hair. The stranger held himself almost regally in the saddle and his gaze followed Sam on to the boardwalk.

'Help you, mister?' Sam asked when the man kept staring at him. He got the impression there was an effort at intimidation behind that gaze, but since he didn't know the fellow he'd give him the benefit of the doubt.

'Maybe you can, Marshal. I'm new in town. Came to visit an old friend of mine. You familiar with most of the people here?'

Sam noticed a soft Southern accent. 'Mostly. Who you lookin' for?'

'Woman by the name of Althea Williams. She's a colored woman.'

A quiver of apprehension went through the marshal. He had the sudden notion something was brewing for her. Something dangerous. She

had been running from something
and though she had never told him
what it was he got the impression she
felt it would catch up to her one day.
Could this stranger be that something?
He surveyed the man, getting nothing
from him except possibly the look of
a man used to imposing his will on
others. Perhaps a businessman, used to
giving orders.

He noted the man's looks, freezing
them in his mind. Later he would
check with Miss Althea on it.

' 'Fraid I don't know her, stranger.'
He kept his voice steady.

The man studied at him, gaze
narrowing, clearly not liking the answer.
'I don't imagine there are too many
slaves in these parts, Marshal. Surely
you've — '

'No more slaves, Mister. Haven't
you heard? There was a war fought
over it.'

The man's lips drew tight and his
eyes glittered and Sam knew he had
done the right thing putting the fellow

off until he could talk to the girl. 'Well, then, I guess I have been misinformed. I shall wire home and find out.' He gave a curt nod.

'You do that, mister.' Sam gave him a brisk tip of the hat and walked into his office, peering out and watching as the man rode away.

★ ★ ★

'He matches those bullets, Luther, we got a problem,' said Jed, leaning hard on the table as they watched the marshal walk out. Bart began to draw his gun but Luther placed a hand over his, forcing it back.

'No, not here,' he said. 'I don't want this many witnesses.'

'But, Luther, those bullets will match sure as hell. He'll be back and we'll have no choice.'

Luther scoffed. 'Hell, we always got a choice, Bart. Sometimes it just takes some lookin' to find it.'

'What you got in mind?' asked Jed.

Luther's eyes hardened. 'Marshal just made a fool of me, Jed. Can't abide that. I was hoping to shoot him when he tried to stop the hold-up, but he matches those bullets it'll interfere with the plan.' Luther paused, running a finger over his lip. 'You do it, Jed. Get him in his office and make sure the deputy or no one else don't see you.'

'You bet, Luther. I been itchin' to do some killin'.'

Luther chuckled 'Ain't we all, Jed. Ain't we all.'

9

Althea set out a plate of sourdough biscuits and started a pot of fresh Arbuckle's to brewing. Matt took a biscuit and tore off a hunk, savoring its sweet taste before swallowing. The dark woman finished frying bacon and eggs, which he devoured with a hunger he hadn't felt in ages, washing them down with a cup of coffee.

The sun streamed through the kitchen windows, warming the room. Everything looked shiny and new and he couldn't recollect a day he'd ever felt this happy about anything. His feelings for her temporarily drove away the grief and fear, dispelled some of the darkness his soul had been trapped by for so long. Nothing had changed outright. The threat of Luther Hinton still hung over him like a black cloud but now he had a reason to go on. He had Althea and suddenly little else mattered. The night he had spent in her arms, safe and protected from the ghosts of the past, was the happiest hc'd ever experienced. She made him feel things he never thought he could, an out-pouring of warmth and splendid emotion; for the first time in his life he had really *lived* and nothing – *nothing* – could take that away from him. Not Luther Hinton or his men, not the losses he had suffered. While dread and grief still existed, emptiness did not. If the tenderness and love in her dark eyes were any indication, he knew she felt the same.

'First time I've seen you smile that way.' Althea smiled herself, a deep warm smile, uninhibited and honest.

'Show that much?' He took a sip of coffee.

Her smile broadened and she smoothed her apron. 'Shows enough to make me happy.'

'I've never felt this way before, Althea. I swear to the Lord above I haven't. I want to spend the rest of my life with you.'

Her eyes widened. 'That sounds suspiciously like a proposal of marriage, Mr Brenner.' She winked. 'A gentleman should be on his knees when he asks that.'

He grinned. 'Reckon it might be a proposal. Never thought about askin' a lady that question before. Might not know it if it snuck up and bit me.'

'It just did.' She giggled and he reckoned that was the first time he had heard her laugh. It was a sweet sound, almost as sweet as her shanties.

He remained silent a moment and the glow faded as darkness drifted over him, the cold storm of reality. Luther Hinton. How could he ever hope to marry Althea, live a normal life with the outlaw still alive?

'What is it, Matt?' Concern shown in her dark eyes. Coming over to him she placed her hand over his.

'There's a damn good chance I won't live long enough to marry you, Althea.

I want nothin' more, but Luther's got other ideas. I don't reckon I'll get the jump on him this time. He don't make many mistakes.'

'Hush!' she said with a curt wave of her hand. 'Don't you talk that way! We could go away, far from here, start over. I've done it before and I'm willin' to do it now.'

Matt slowly shook his head. 'That ain't the way and you know it, Althea. We'd just be runnin' again and it's time to stop that. We'd never have a day without fear of him or Carter findin' us if we did.'

'I know.' Her gaze dropped. 'Reckon I knew it all long but I let myself hope again.'

'Hope's the best I can give you.'

She looked up, face turning serious. 'Please, Matt, go to the marshal. You can't face those men alone. I won't let you.'

He sighed. He'd been mulling the notion over in his mind since she first brought it up and the way he saw it it would make little difference. It all came down to proof. 'Told you it likely won't do a lick of good.'

She squeezed his forearm. 'You don't know that. Maybe he can help. At least you'll have someone by your side, an extra gun.'

He stood, gripping her arms. 'I don't want you involved in this, Althea. I mean that. I didn't fall in love with you just to lose you like I lost everybody else in my life.'

'I'm already involved, Matt. You think Luther will let me alone once he has you? He won't and you know it. He ain't that kind of man. He's just like Carter in some ways, though without the refinement. He's cold-blooded and mean as a scorpion. He'll kill me too. I knew he would the moment I made the decision to fetch the marshal and come to the saloon. And I accepted the risk. I think I loved you the first time I saw you, Matt, and there ain't much point to my life with you dead. That means I'll stand by your side, dead or alive.'

Matt turned away, walking into the parlor, dread in his soul. She was right; there was no arguing it. Luther would kill her and he couldn't let that happen. But how could he prevent it? How could he get to Luther first, bring the outlaw down before Luther got him? Confusion rose in his mind. Before it had been so easy, when he bought the gun. He would kill Luther, somehow, let his lust for revenge rage enough to do what needed to be done. But now . . . now he had Althea, a reason to live, and that complicated matters more than he had planned. But there were facts to face: Luther would come for him, and soon. Damn soon. What could one man do against the likes of the Scarred L Gang? Damn little, and risking his own life was one thing, but risking hers . . .

Perhaps she was right. The marshal was only one man but he had a deputy and together maybe they could come up with something, arrange a posse of enough locals to thwart the outlaw, bring him to justice. One thing he vowed: Luther would never stand trial. Succeed or fail, Luther would die by Matt's hand for what he had done. Matt would never have that ghost in his nightmares again.

Althea walked into the room, coming up behind him and gently laying a hand on his shoulder. 'There's a way, Matt. Trust me. There has to be. I haven't come this far to lose it all now either.'

He turned to her. 'I'll go to the marshal, Althea. I'll tell him all I know. I'm tired of facing this alone.'

'You ain't alone, not no more. Neither of us are.'

He kissed her deeply, overwhelmed with emotion. He wished Luther Hinton had never existed, that he had met Althea years ago, before he met up with the Scarred L Gang. But he couldn't change what was and all the wishing in the world wouldn't help a damn. There was only confronting his mistakes, striking hard and fast, before

Luther got himself set.

As he pulled away he peered into her dark eyes. 'Load the Spencer, Althea. Keep it ready while I'm gone. I don't know if Luther will try anything but I ain't willin' to take the chance.'

She nodded and he turned to the door, grabbing his hat from the wall peg. 'Wait.' She hurried into her room and returned a few seconds later with a small red-flannel bag. The bag was sewn to a leather thong tied at one end to make a necklace. She placed it over his head and kissed him.

'What is this?' He took it between his fingers, feeling of the soft material.

'It's a charm I made when I was a slave. Wore it for luck. Gave me hope that freedom was comin'. Ain't needed it in two years but I reckon you need it now.'

He smiled, nodding and going to the door. 'I'll come back, Althea, don't you worry.'

'I will just the same.'

He kissed her again and put on his

hat. 'Load that rifle.'

After he left, she gently closed the door and leaned heavily against it. A tear slipped down her cheek.

★ ★ ★

Rico watched as Matt Brenner departed the woman's home. The outlaw smiled. The smile was something of evil, wanton thoughts, and he imagined what he would do to the dark woman when he burst in. She was in for a treat with ol' Rico, yes she was. A sweet *señorita* like that.

His gaze followed the boy along the street; Brenner was heading towards the marshal's office. A flicker of suspicion rose in his mind. What was the boy doing? Was he going to ask the marshal's help? Wasn't like the Matt Brenner he had known five years ago, but, hell, a fella had a right to change in that amount of time, 'less of course you rode with Luther then you best not set your sights on anything but following orders. The boy went into the office and closed the door. After a moment's consideration, Rico's gaze returned to the woman's homestead. Let Luther worry about Brenner. Rico had other concerns. A snake of drool slithered from the corner of his blistered lips as he thought about her. Yes, it was finally time, time for Rico to pay her a call.

He straightened, checking the street to make sure no one was paying him any particular attention. He hesitated when he noticed a stranger looking up and down the street; the fella stopped a woman passing by and asked her something, then glanced in the direction of Althea Williams' house. Wondering, Rico waited a moment, until the man's attention turned away, passing it off as nothing to worry about.

He scooted across the street, a vicious grin turning his lips and his hand sliding over the butt of his gun.

★ ★ ★

Althea mouthed a silent a prayer Matt would come back to her alive and wiped the tear from her cheek. She had seen the recklessness in his eyes mellow and she knew she had given him a reason to go on, as he had her. But would that mean anything where the likes of Luther Hinton was concerned? She wondered. Perhaps Matt would be overpowered by his rage, perhaps her love wasn't enough.

Deep fear began to well inside her again, a fear she had experienced far too much of in her life. A fear of loss, of something slipping through your fingers, being taken from you, something you had no way of stopping. Carter had taken her son and her pride and now Luther Hinton might take the only man she'd ever loved. She trembled with the fear, nearly overwhelmed, then gripped her composure, knowing fretting about such things would do no good. What would happen would happen, and at least Matt had agreed to fetch help. And despite his arguments, she would be there by his side when he faced Hinton. She would be there with the Spencer and by the Lord above she would kill the outlaw if she had the chance.

A sound took her from her thoughts and she tensed, listening, wondering if she had heard anything at all. Yes, she felt sure she had. A scuffing sound, as if someone had stepped on to her porch.

Matt? No, he had gone to the marshal's; it would not be him. Who then?

You're scarin' yourself silly, child! That's all it is! It ain't nothin'. Street's full of sounds this time of morning!

Why couldn't she convince herself of that? The fear inside her strengthened and she suddenly recollected what Matt told her about loading the Spencer.

She went to a small desk in the corner and opened a drawer, locating a box of shells. Two in hand — that's all she'd ever owned, having had no opportunity to fire the Spencer since she stole it two years ago — she went to the wall and took the rifle from the rack, loading it.

Going to the window she peered cautiously out, scanning the front. She saw nothing.

Or did she?

Was there a hint of movement there? A blur of clothing? Her face pinched and her hands bleached as she clutched the Spencer more tightly. She breathed staggered breaths and stepped away from the window, edging towards the door, intending to open it and have a look.

It's nothing, she told herself. Nothing at all.

But her belly plunged with fear as she took another step toward the door, pulling back the Spencer's hammer just in case. She prayed the gun still worked after all this time. Though she had told Matt it did, she couldn't be sure because she hadn't fired it in more than two years.

The question was suddenly answered for her. The door burst inward, propelled by a crashing kick. It rebounded from the wall and she froze, mouth dropping open, a chill shivering through her body.

A man filled the doorway, one she recognized, one of Luther's men, the one called Rico. He had a look on his face that sent a wave of terror through her, one she had seen on the face of Dale Carter far too many times when he came to her room late at night — the look of men who liked to hurt before killing. He had a Smith & Wesson in one hand.

She let out a gasp and jerked the Spencer up, intending to give the man no opportunity to hurt her. She had no qualms about killing him because he would kill her or Matt in an instant and suddenly he was all her demons of the past bundled into one man.

The outlaw grinned, lunged, swinging

an arm and knocking the Spencer sideways just as she pulled the trigger.

The hammer clacked but no shot sounded. The shells were bad! The gun didn't work! As the thoughts locked in her mind she tried to reverse the rifle and use the butt as a club.

Rico swept his free arm up and caught the Spencer in mid-swing. He jerked, wrenching it from her grip and hurling it aside.

Terror crossing her face, she backed up, mind scrambling for a way to escape the outlaw, who advanced on her like a stalking animal. Her eyes widened as he levelled his gun.

A shot sounded.

★ ★ ★

Matt walked towards the marshal's office, a glimmer of hope in his mind. The threat hadn't changed but his perspective had. Perhaps the marshal could do nothing without proof but at least Matt would have a better chance with two. His main concern was Althea. He hadn't told her but he was going to the marshal for more than just his help with Luther Hinton. He wanted his help with another matter: protection. At all costs he wanted Althea protected and the marshal could provide that by sending a deputy to guard her. Of course Matt would have to come clean with everything he knew about Hinton and the Scarred L Gang, including his own involvement with them, but he saw little choice at this point.

As long as Althea was out of danger.

He glanced at the saloon a bit farther on, wondering what Luther Hinton was doing, thinking, planning. Peacemaker at his hip, Matt could so easily walk in there and just start shooting. But there were three other men with him and one of them would surely put a bullet in him. Two days ago he wouldn't have cared. But now . . .

He had made Althea a promise and he would keep it.

He crossed the street, throwing a

glance at a blond-haired man standing just down the way, asking something of a woman. He couldn't recall ever having seen the fella before. Strangers so rarely came to Hopespring.

A sudden pang of dread stabbed his belly and he wondered why. Perhaps it was just everything coming together after all these years, perhaps it was worry about the woman he'd come to love.

Shrugging it off, he shifted his gaze to the marshal's office and stepped onto the boardwalk, going to the door.

Entering, he stopped just inside the door, an uneasy feeling sending a chill down his spine.

Something felt *wrong*. The feeling struck him immediately and his gaze shifted to the marshal's desk. It was empty, but an ominous stillness hung in the air, something unnatural, and it gave him a sinking feeling; he had felt it too many times before. It was the feeling of death.

And death had visited this room

It took him only an instant to pinpoint its source. A puddle, dark and shiny, crept outward from behind the desk, reflecting glints of sunlight.

Matt felt his insides tighten and he swallowed hard. A raw coppery scent hung heavy in the air. Taking a step, his legs felt as if he'd been in the saddle for three days, but he forced himself to go around the desk and look.

He froze, pressing his eyes shut, slowly opening them again. Blood. Everywhere. Puddled and flowing. Death *had* visited this room and very recently.

He knelt, hand edging out, fingers trembling, and touched the body of Marshal Sam Johnson. He turned the lawman towards him, seeing the shirt soaked with blood, the hole in the man's chest. No life was left in the marshal, that took only a second to determine. In the marshal's open hand were six bullets.

A prickle of dread skittered down his back. A thought, a warning, struggled to

241

form in his mind. The bullets . . . what did they mean?

Something left undone. Whichever member of the gang had killed the marshal had come with a purpose and those bullets were it. But they were still in the marshal's hand.

Realization hit Matt suddenly then and he froze an instant with the thought: the body was fresh and the bullets were still here. That could only mean one thing!

He slowly straightened, an icy wave sweeping through the hairs on the back of his neck.

The *skritch* of a hammer being drawn back stopped him before he could turn around.

The bullets were in the marshal's hand because the killer was still here! That's what Matt had felt when he walked in — the man's presence!

A motion at his hip; he felt his Peacemaker lifted from its holster. The man holding the gun to his back hurled the Peacemaker and it landed in one of the cells across the room.

'Fancy time for you to be showin' up here, Brenner,' said the man. 'Turn around, slow-like.'

Matt complied, turning to look into the grinning features of Jed Hinton.

10

Luther Hinton, followed by his brother Bart, stepped into the marshal's office. Closing the door, Luther glanced at Jed, who held his Smith & Wesson aimed at Matt's chest.

Jed slipped behind Matt and plucked the bullets from the dead marshal's hand, passing them to Luther, who dropped them in his duster pocket.

'Looks like this is almost finished, boy.' The outlaw stepped deeper into the room.

'Why did you kill him?' Matt asked through tight lips. 'He didn't have nothin' to do with this.'

Luther gave an indifferent chuckle. 'Beg to differ, boy. Seems his deputy found that old shopkeep where we hid 'im. He had the bullets from my gun. Was gonna match them. So you see, I had to kill him. I ain't in the habit of leavin' witnesses, least ones who're lawmen.'

Matt felt his belly plunge. He had no chance now. He was in the hands of the killer and soon it would be over. He had no way to protect himself, let alone Althea.

Luther walked to the window, glancing out at the street, then turning back to Matt. Jed and Bart stood in the centre of the room, guns levelled. Matt wondered where Rico was, and vague fear rose in his mind.

'Where's the Mex?' he asked suddenly, the fear overwhelming him, and Luther laughed.

'Why he's gone to pay your lady friend a visit. You know how much he likes the ladies.'

Matt felt all hope drain from his soul. He recollected what Rico had done to a couple of Kansas whores and shuddered. The thought burning in his mind, he considered taking his chances, charging Luther, trying to get his gun. Jed and Bart would gun him down instantly, but did it matter? He saw no way out of this alive and the thought of the Mex with Althea made his blood run cold.

Something held him back, a specter of past decisions. He had always charged ahead, never thought things through; he might be repeating that mistake if he rushed Luther now. While he saw no options, he didn't move, alert for the slightest drop in the outlaw's guard, the slightest mistake. His gaze shifted to the other men, whose faces showed little emotion beyond a vague vicious expectation. They would have preferred to kill him right there, but Luther was waiting. Why? Was there more to his plan? Maybe that would mean a chance to save Althea.

Matt's gaze swept back to the outlaw as Luther stepped up to him. Matt didn't like the look in his eyes. 'Decided to be fair about this, boy. Gonna give you another chance to join up with the Scarred L Gang.'

'You go to hell!' Matt held Luther's

gaze, refusing to back down.

'Reckoned you'd see it that way, but I ain't givin' you a choice, not if you got a notion of keepin' that gal alive.'

Matt's belly tightened, but he couldn't stop the twinge of hope that went through him. 'What do you mean?'

'You messed up my plan, boy. Didn't expect you to walk in on Jed. Was gonna let you find that cuffy of yours all done up nice, way only Rico can. I wanted to see you suffer 'fore you died. But that's changed, now.' The outlaw's brow crinkled and he ran a finger over his upper lip. 'Told Rico not to touch her 'less I came and gave the order. I'm a fair man. You do me a little favor and I'll set her free.'

Was the outlaw lying? Matt looked deep into his horseshoe-colored eyes, dead eyes, eyes filled with evil, corruption. It was hard to tell when Luther lied; the outlaw was a master at deceit. 'What makes you think I'd believe you?'

'I'm a man of my word, boy, you know that.'

'You're a cold-blooded bastard, that's as much as I know. Any sense of honor you might have had is long since gone.'

Luther gave a sarcastic chuckle. 'Hurt that you'd feel that way, boy, but you owe me. I don't cotton to backin' down and now you're gonna make up for it.' Luther, pausing, walked away, then turned back and placed his hand on the butt of his gun. 'I want the money you been sendin' that woman. It's mine. Ain't about to leave without it. I know you won't give it to me so I aim to take it and some extra from the bank. You're gonna help. Maybe then I'll consider your debt paid.'

Matt peered at him with suspicion and confusion. The outlaw had something in his mind, what? 'You never considered a debt paid.'

'Will this time.' Luther's features

darkened. 'You're gonna help us rob the bank, boy. One for old time's sake, you could say.'

Shock welded on to Matt's face and his insides froze.

Nooo, please don't shoot — I got a wife and kids!

The nightmare memory of the bank hold-up in Kansas flashed through his mind and with crashing dread he saw the utter deviousness of Luther's plan. Luther had pinpointed the thing that haunted Matt the most and now he would use it. But, if he knew Luther, there was more to it than that.

'See you like my plan, boy. You'll help us rob that bank, just the way you did five years ago. When it's over, you're free to go.'

'I don't believe you.'

'You don't have to. Makes no never mind to me.'

'I won't help you, Luther. My bank-robbin' days are finished.'

'Oh, you'll help, or Rico'll have your lady friend all to himself. You know how hard he can be on a gal. Ain't a-many that are the same after and them whores are used to rough treatment. Your lady friend don't strike me quite as durable.'

Matt cringed inside. He had no choice. Luther was lying, he felt sure, but if there was even a chance he would let Althea live Matt had to take it.

'Appears I got no choice,' Matt said at last, defeat in his tone.

'That's for damn sure.' Luther then did something unexpected. He lifted the Smith & Wesson from its holster and held it out before him, offering it to Matt. Matt stared in disbelief. 'Take it, boy. Can't rob a bank without a gun.'

Matt tentatively reached out, taking the revolver. In the same movement, he spun it around and brought it up, levelling on Luther's head. Fanning the hammer, he jerked the trigger. The hammer fell on empty chambers.

Luther laughed. 'What kind of fool

you take me for? Think I'd trust you with a loaded gun?'

Matt stared stupidly at the empty Smith & Wesson in his hand while the outlaws laughed.

Luther motioned and the men pulled bandannas over their lower faces. None offered Matt a mask. Luther motioned for Bart to give him his gun and the brother passed it over with a slightly puzzled look.

'Don't worry, Bart, you won't need it. We got an extra member, remember?' Bart chuckled and Matt saw a look pass between them. 'Where'd that deputy get off to, anyhow? Can't leave any loose ends.'

'Saw him head into the bank a few minutes ago.' Bart smiled.

Luther nodded, raising an eyebrow. 'Good, that'll make it all nice and tidy. Reckon that'll make this extra special for you, boy.' Luther's gaze settled on Matt. 'Another dead deputy, 'cept this time you won't be sendin' no money to his family.'

Luther motioned and the brothers moved towards the door, opening it and filing out into the street. Passers-by shot the masked men looks, cast Matt looks as well, but quickly scattered as the men walked along the street.

Luther prodded Matt on ahead of him, the brothers taking point. 'Just like old times, boy, just like old times. I'd planned on waitin' to rob the bank till a little later, but you showin' up at the marshal's office made things easy for me. Saw you go in from the saloon and figured you'd stumble across Jed here. Worked out well, doncha think?'

Matt didn't answer. He stared straight ahead at the bank, remembering a time years ago when he had made this same journey. Remembering the coldness, the fear, and remembering the aftermath.

Help me! Don't let him kill me!

The words shuddered hollowly in his memory and he saw the deputy's death over and over in his mind. It was happening again. The deputy would be there, a man he knew well, a friend, a man with a wife and baby daughter. And he would die, as that deputy died five years ago. Again Matt would be responsible. This time, however, he would have no opportunity to feel guilt, for Luther would see to it Matt died in the robbery. That was the rest of his plan; that's why he had given him the empty gun.

They walked up to the bank doors, Bart and Jed shoving them open and stepping in, shouting, Jed waving his gun in the air. Customers, a handful of them, froze, looks of terror hitting their faces.

Luther jabbed Matt in the back with his gun barrel, forcing him in. He saw the deputy standing over to the side, talking with the bank manager. The man looked up, a look of vague confusion and shock on his face as he eyed the masked men, then settled his gaze on Matt, perplexity deepening.

Matt said a silent prayer. It was the only thing left to do. Sweat trickled down his face, sides. His heart pounded.

Luther moved around to Matt's side.

Bart and Jed menaced the customers into a tight group by the vault door.

'Put all the money in bags,' Jed ordered a teller behind the cage. The teller hesitated and Jed triggered a shot that gouged a chunk of wood from the counter. The man, trembling, grabbed a canvas bag and began stuffing it with bills.

Luther's gaze scanned the bank, settling briefly on the deputy, who didn't move. He knew he was out-gunned.

Luther looked at Matt, who stood helpless, hand welded to the empty Smith & Wesson. 'Hold your gun up, boy. You can't make a point with it aimed at your goddamned feet.' He chuckled and began to swing his revolver towards the deputy.

The deputy's face took on a startled look, a knowing look, a look of death.

Luther glanced at Matt, whose face

twisted in horror.

The deputy's hand swept for his gun. He knew in a moment he would die and had nothing to lose by drawing.

Nooo, please don't shoot — I got a wife and kids!

The words shuddered through Matt's memory.

Luther brought his gun level.

The deputy drew a beat too slow.

Time seemed to stop. Matt, desperate, screamed and lunged at Luther!

It was the only thing left to do. He would die anyway.

Luther Hinton, off-balance, fired. The shot thundered through the bank and the slug ripped into the deputy's shoulder, kicking him into a backward stumble.

Luther twisted to meet Matt's attack and Matt swung the empty gun. The outlaw ducked and the gun sailed past his shoulder.

As Matt struggled to regain his equilibrium, Luther turned the gun in his direction.

Across the floor both brothers turned, stunned by the sudden turn of events.

The deputy regained his footing and his hand again went for the Peacemaker at his hip.

Vicious lights danced in Luther's eyes as he brought his gun to aim on Matt's chest.

A shot blasted.

Luther's face washed blank and he jolted, a slug from the deputy's gun punching into his side.

With pure instinct Matt acted, throwing a looping punch that took the outlaw clean across the jaw. Luther staggered, losing his hold on his Smith & Wesson and stuttering a step backward.

The deputy triggered another shot, this time at Bart, whose face dropped with shock as he looked down to find a gushing hole in his chest. The Hinton brother collapsed into a heap, blood spilling across the floor.

The second brother went into action, jerking his gun towards the deputy.

Two customers leaped at Jed from behind, bringing him down before he could fire. They beat him with fists until the brother lay still, blood running from his scalp, nose and lips.

Matt charged Luther again, swinging as he came in. The outlaw had recovered his balance, but was bleeding liberally from his side, hunching slightly to his left. He still had plenty of strength left, however, and avoided Matt's blow, throwing a punch of his own that caught Matt in the teeth. The blow rattled him, making his legs go rubbery and Luther hit him again.

The room whirled and Matt went down. He hit the floor hard and struggled to get back up, shaking his head to clear the cobwebs.

Luther delivered a kick to Matt's side. Bile rose in Matt's throat and he swallowed against it, groaning, ribs throbbing.

Luther brought his foot up to stamp on Matt's head, a blow that would end his struggle permanently.

Beneath him, something, poking into his side.

The outlaw's Smith & Wesson! He had landed on it!

He twisted, clenching the weapon and rolling, triggering a shot as he came up on his side. The shot took Luther square in the chest and hurled him backward. The outlaw crashed against the wall, sliding down in an exaggerated motion.

Matt, breath staggering out, forced himself to his feet, gun in hand in case Luther regrouped. There was no need. Luther gasped liquidy breaths; blood streamed from his mouth. Matt peered down at him and the outlaw's horseshoe eyes tried to focus on him.

'Son . . . ofabitch . . . ' he muttered, and the lights in his eyes blinked out.

It was over. All the years of wondering when Luther Hinton would return to collect his due, all the pain and guilt and fear. Over. Luther Hinton was dead, as was his gang, with the possible exception of Jed, who might

survive the beating he had taken.
And Rico.

A chill washed through Matt's body. *Rico*! He was with Althea!

Matt checked the load in his gun, finding three bullets left. That would be enough. He whirled to see the deputy coming up beside him.

'Matt?'

Matt shook his head. 'Marshal's dead. This is the Scarred L Gang, the ones who killed him. They forced me to come along with them.'

The deputy nodded, taking Matt's word for it.

'There's one more,' he added, starting for the door.

'I'll come with you.'

Matt glanced at the deputy's bleeding shoulder and shook his head. 'Best get yourself some attention. I have to do this alone.'

The deputy peered at him, but nodded and Matt threw open the door and ran.

It was over, but one loose end

remained, one reminder of the past. Rico, a vicious outlaw who threatened Althea's life.

He ran along the boardwalk, heart thundering, sweat pouring down his face, breath beating out. He kept the Smith & Wesson in hand, clenching it so hard his hand turned white. The unforeseeable had happened — Luther Hinton was dead, his menace ended forever. But if he lost Althea now that would matter little to him.

He reached her house, stopping short as he saw the door hanging open.

Panting, he shuddered with dread as he peered into the house, afraid he would find her, or what was left of her after Rico had finished, lying in blood on the floor.

Instead he found Rico.

The outlaw lay on the parlor floor, a gun clutched in his lifeless fingers. The back of his head was missing.

Matt knelt beside the outlaw, brow crinkling. It made no sense. Althea wouldn't have shot him in the back of the head and left him here.

He straightened, an ominous feeling penetrating his soul, the same feeling he had felt upon entering the marshal's office earlier. Something was wrong. Dead wrong.

'Althea?' he yelled, suddenly taking a step forward. 'Althea, where are you?'

A scream came in answer!

'Matt, get out!' he heard her call from the bedroom. He tensed, rushing forward and stepping into the room.

He saw her immediately. She lay on the floor, blood running from her swollen lips and nose, tears tracking from her eyes. Her blouse was torn open and her skirt was bloodied. Her hair was dishevelled and he could tell she had gone through hell.

But Rico was dead.

She saw him then, and made a move to say something.

He never got the chance to hear what it was.

Something hard collided with the back of his head and the gun flew from his fingers. It spun across the floor as he stumbled deeper into the room.

The surroundings spun and he fought to orient himself. Someone had been standing behind the door, had hit him, but who?

Rico's killer.

He had no time to dwell on it. As he staggered forward, trying to turn, he caught a flash of gunmetal streaking towards his head and tried to sidestep, but wasn't completely successful. The butt clacked from the side of his face and a curtain of stars exploded across his vision. His legs deserted him and he stumbled against the bed, leaning half on the edge. Through blurred vision he saw the man, recognizing him — the stranger he had noticed talking to the woman on the street earlier. Dazed, he didn't understand why the man was here, what he could possibly want.

The man uttered a laugh and holstered his gun. He stepped over to Matt and lifted him, hurling him sideways into a wall. Matt slammed into it, breath exploding from his lungs, and the man was on him again, giving him no chance to recover.

The blond-haired man hit him with a fist and Matt's head snapped back. Blood ran from his lip. The fellow didn't let up; he kept hitting, pounding, and Matt took three blows in a row, powerless to protect himself. His senses started to desert him and he heard a distant ringing in his brain. He barely felt the next blow, though his entire body shuddered with its impact.

A shot broke the assault.

Matt stared, stunned, at the man, whose face took on a shocked, strangely betrayed look. The man uttered a choppy sound that might have been a laugh of defiance. He dropped to the floor, a hole in his back gouting blood.

For endless moments Matt stared down at the man, unable to move, breath stuttering out in hot ragged gasps, vision blurred. As his sight cleared, he saw the fellow clearly and realization burst into his mind.

Dale Carter! It had to be. The man who had held Althea captive all those years, the man who had taken her son from her, taken her self-respect. Matt didn't understand how the man had come to be here and killed Rico and he didn't care. All that mattered was he was dead and two ghosts had met their doom today.

He looked over to see the gun, the Smith & Wesson he had lost, dropping from Althea's grip. A new burst of tears streaked down her face, mixing with blood and dripping from her chin.

'He showed up just after Rico came in . . . ' she said, voice shaky, low. 'He shot him, then he . . . then he took me in here and started to hurt me . . . '

Matt pushed himself from the wall, going to her, helping her to her feet. He held her while tears soaked his shoulder.

★ ★ ★

A month passed and all that had happened with Luther Hinton seemed like a distant dark dream to Matt. As he stepped into the parlor, shutting the door behind him, the events replayed in his mind, because today would be the day it became a memory for good. Jed Hinton had lived just long enough to see the end of a rope. The deputy had recovered from his wound and was acting as marshal and Matt reckoned the job couldn't have gone to a braver man.

He had regrets a-many, as well as guilt for ever joining Hinton's gang in the first place. All could have been avoided had he just had a lick of sense: John and Tim would still be alive, the marshal, Mr Fuller. But he couldn't change the past. All that mattered was the future and not making the mistakes again. He would have to live with what had happened but he would fear it no more. He prayed the dead could forgive him.

He would continue to send money

to the deputy's wife in Kansas every third Monday until it ran out, then he would consider the debt satisfied if not repaid.

Dale Carter was another story. He had died at Althea's hands and Matt had worried for a time how she would accept killing a man. She seemed relieved in a way, knowing he would haunt her no more, that she was finally free, but he had seen the sorrow in her dark eyes as well. Killing a man was a hell of a thing and she would have to live with that in her own way.

He'd decided to rebuild the farm, somehow, start again. He still had the horses the livery man was holding, some of which he had sold off to pay his debt, and he would sell a few others to start rebuilding. The bank man, grateful for Matt's help in thwarting the robbery, had offered to help out with a loan. John and Tim would want it that way, he felt sure. He owed them — and himself — that much.

That left only two pieces of unfinished business, both of which he'd attend to now.

'Althea?' he yelled. She came from the kitchen, slapping flour-covered hands on her apron and smiling.

'Matt, you weren't s'posed to be home for hours, not till after you wired the money and finished up with the loan at the bank.'

He smiled a warm smile. 'Had me somethin' more important to do first.'

She gazed at him, brow crinkling. 'What could be more important than that?'

'I took me a little of the money from the horse sales and went to the jewelry shop.'

Her dark eyes brightened.

He went to her, dropping to one knee and looking up. 'A spell ago you told me a gentleman should ask for a lady's hand on his knees. Well, I'm askin' you now. Marry me, Althea Williams.' He took a box from his pocket and opened it, taking out a small diamond ring and sliding it on her finger. She gazed at it, eyes glossing with tears.

'You know I will, Mr Brenner. You know I will!'

He stood, kissing her deeply. 'This calls for a celebration.' He undid the ties of her apron and let it drop to the floor, then took her hand and guided her towards the door.

'Where we goin', Matt? I still got biscuits to finish!'

'They can wait.'

He opened the door and pulled her outside.

Two horses stood in front of the house, one his own, which he'd brought from the livery. The other was a bay, who nickered contentedly as the eight-year-old boy atop its saddle petted her mane.

Althea's face went pale as she saw the dark-skinned child. 'Matt . . . ' A whisper, trembling.

He smiled, emotion balling in his throat. 'Took a little work. Had a friend run a check on all the homes in the Springfield area. They found him at one. He wired me about it two weeks ago and I wired the home about the circumstances. They agreed to let him come out to see you. I met him at the stage today. You just got to sign some papers and make things official.'

Tears streaked down Althea's face and she ran to the boy, pulling him out of the saddle and into her arms. Matt watched as she sobbed with joy and went to them, hugging them both.

THE END

**Other titles in the
Linford Western Library**

THE CROOKED SHERIFF
John Dyson

Black Pete Bowen quit Texas with a burning hatred of men who try to take the law into their own hands. But he discovers that things aren't much different in the silver mountains of Arizona.

THEY'LL HANG BILLY FOR SURE:
Larry & Stretch
Marshall Grover

Billy Reese, the West's most notorious desperado, was to stand trial. From all compass points came the curious and the greedy, the riff-raff of the frontier. Suddenly, a crazed killer was on the loose — but the Texas Trouble-Shooters were there, girding their loins for action.

RIDERS OF RIFLE RANGE
Wade Hamilton

Veterinarian Jeff Jones did not like open warfare — but it was there on Scrub Pine grass. When he diagnosed a sick bull on the Endicott ranch as having the contagious blackleg disease, he got involved in the warfare — whether he liked it or not!

BEAR PAW
Nevada Carter

Austin Dailey traded two cows to a pair of Indians for a bay horse, which subsequently disappeared. Tracks led to a secret hideout of fugitive Indians — and cattle thieves. Indians and stockmen co-operated against the rustlers. But it was Pale Woman who acted as interpreter between her people and the rangemen.

THE WEST WITCH
Lance Howard

Detective Quinton Hilcrest journeys west, seeking the Black Hood Bandits' lost fortune. Within hours of arriving in Hags Bend, he is fighting for his life, ensnared with a beautiful outcast the town claims is a witch! Can he save the young woman from the angry mob?

GUNS OF THE PONY EXPRESS
T. M. Dolan

Rich Zennor joined the Pony Express venture at the start, as second-in-command to tough Denning Hartman. But Zennor had the problems of Hartman believing that they had crossed trails in the past, and the fact that he was strongly attached to Hartman's Indian girl, Conchita.

BLACK JO OF THE PECOS
Jeff Blaine

Nobody knew where Black Josephine Callard came from or whither she returned. Deputy U.S. Marshal Frank Haggard would have to exercise all his cunning and ability to stay alive before he could defeat her highly successful gang and solve the mystery.

RIDE FOR YOUR LIFE
Johnny Mack Bride

They rode west, hoping for a new start. Then they met another broken-down casualty of war, and he had a plan that might deliver them from despair. But the only men who would attempt it would be the truly brave — or the desperate. They were both.

THE NIGHTHAWK
Charles Burnham

While John Baxter sat looking at the ruin that arsonists had made of his log house, a stranger rode into the yard. Baxter and Walt Showalter partnered up and re-built the house. But when it was dynamited, they struck back — and all hell broke loose.

MAVERICK PREACHER
M. Duggan

Clay Purnell was hopeful that his posting to Capra would be peaceable enough. However, on his very first day in town he rode into trouble. Although loath to use his .45, Clay found he had little choice — and his likeness to a notorious bank robber didn't help either!

SIXGUN SHOWDOWN
Art Flynn

After years as a lawman elsewhere, Dan Herrick returned to his old Arizona stamping ground to find that nesters were being driven from their homesteads by ruthless ranchers. Before putting away his gun once and for all, Dan forced a bloody and decisive showdown.

RIDE LIKE THE DEVIL!
Sam Gort

Ben Trunch arrived back on the Big T only to find that land-grabbing was in progress. He confronted Luke Fletcher, saloon-keeper and town boss, with what was happening, and was immediately forced to ride for his life. But he got the chance to put it all right in the end.

SLOW WOLF AND DAN FOX:
Larry & Stretch
Marshall Grover

The deck was stacked against an innocent man. Larry Valentine played detective, and his investigation propelled the Texas Trouble-Shooters into a gun-blazing fight to the finish.

BRANAGAN'S LAW
Alan Irwin

To Angus Flint, the valley was his domain and he didn't want any new settlers. But Texas Ranger Jim Branagan had other ideas. Could he put an end to Flint's tyranny for good?

THE DEVIL RODE A PINTO
Bret Rey

When a settler is cut to ribbons in a frenzied attack, Texas Ranger Sam Buck learns that the killer is Rufus Berry, known as The Devil. Sam stiffens his resolve to kill or capture Berry and break up his gang.

THE DEATH MAN
Lee F. Gregson
The hardest of men went in fear of Ford, the bounty hunter, who had earned the name 'The Death Man'. Yet even Ford was not infallible — when he killed the wrong man, he found that he was being sought himself by the feared Frank Ambler.

LEAD LANGUAGE
Gene Tuttle
After Blaze Colton and Ricky Rawlings have delivercd a train load of cows from Arizona to San Francisco, they become involved in a load of trouble and find themselves on the run!

A DOLLAR FROM THE STAGE
Bill Morrison
Young saddle-tramp Len Finch stumbled into a web of murder, lawlessness, intrigue and evil ambition. In the end, he put his life on the line for the folks that he cared about.

BRAND 2: HARDCASE
Neil Hunter

When Ben Wyatt and his gang hold up the bank in Adobe, Wyatt is captured. Judge Rice asks Jason Brand, an ex-U.S. Marshal, to take up the silver star. Wyatt is in the cells, his men close by, and Brand is the only man to get Adobe out of real trouble . . .

THE GUNMAN AND THE ACTRESS
Chap O'Keefe

To be paid a heap of money just for protecting a fancy French actress and her troupe of players didn't seem that difficult — but Joshua Dillard hadn't banked on the charms of the actress, and the fact that someone didn't want him even to reach the town . . .

HE RODE WITH QUANTRILL
Terry Murphy
Following the break-up of Quantrill's Raiders, both Jesse James and Mel Becher head their own gang. A decade later, their paths cross again when, unknowingly, they plan to rob the same bank — leading to a violent confrontation between Becher and James.

THE CLOVERLEAF CATTLE COMPANY
Lauran Paine
Bessie Thomas believed in miracles, and her husband, Jawn Henry, did not. But after finding a murdered settler and his woman, and running down the renegades responsible, Jawn Henry would have time to reflect. He and Bessie had never had children. Miracles evidently did happen.

COOGAN'S QUEST
J. P. Weston
Coogan came down from Wyoming on the trail of a man he had vowed to kill — Red Sheene, known as The Butcher. It was the kidnap of Marian De Quincey that gave Coogan his chance — but he was to need help from an unexpected quarter to avoid losing his own life.

DEATH COMES TO ROCK SPRINGS
Steven Gray
Jarrod Kilkline is in trouble with the army, the law, and a bounty hunter. Fleeing from capture, he rescues Brian Tyler, who has been left for dead by the three Jackson brothers. But when the Jacksons reappear on the scene, will Jarrod side with them or with the law in the final showdown?